TWERP

TWERP

Mark Goldblatt

Random House 🏠 New York

Text copyright © 2013 by Mark Goldblatt
Jacket art copyright © 2013 by Joanna Szachowska

All rights reserved. Published in the United States by Random House Children's Books, a division of Random House, Inc., New York.

Random House and the colophon are registered trademarks of Random House, Inc.

Visit us on the Web!
randomhouse.com/kids

Educators and librarians, for a variety of teaching tools, visit us at
RHTeachersLibrarians.com

Library of Congress Cataloging-in-Publication Data
Goldblatt, Mark, 1957–.
Twerp / Mark Goldblatt. — 1st ed.
p. cm.
Summary: In Queens, New York, in 1969, twelve-year-old Julian Twerski writes a journal for his English teacher in which he explores his friendships and how they are affected by girls, a new student who may be as fast as Julian, and especially an incident of bullying.
ISBN 978-0-375-97142-6 (trade) — ISBN 978-0-375-97143-3 (lib. bdg.) — ISBN 978-0-375-97144-0 (ebook)
[1. Friendship—Fiction. 2. Interpersonal relations—Fiction. 3. Self-realization—Fiction. 4. Conduct of life—Fiction. 5. Schools—Fiction. 6. Diaries—Fiction. 7. Queens (New York, N.Y.)—History—20th century—Fiction.] I. Title.
PZ7.G56447Jul 2013 [Fic]—dc23 2012005033

Printed in the United States of America

10 9 8 7 6 5 4 3 2

First Edition

For the Thirty-Fourth Avenue Boys:
Eddy, Larry, Ricky, Joey, David, and Sheldon*

*Don't try to figure out who's who. It won't work.

Julian Twerski   January 11, 1969

The Pigeons of Ponzini

My English teacher, Mr. Selkirk, says I have to write something, and it has to be long, on account of the thing that happened over winter recess— which, in my opinion, doesn't amount to much. It's not like I meant for Danley to get hurt, and I don't think that what happened was one hundred percent my fault, or even a lot my fault, even though I don't deny that I was there. So I guess I deserved to get suspended like the rest of them. I mean, maybe I could've stopped it. *Maybe.* But now the suspension is over, and Selkirk says I've got to write something, and because he says so, my dad says so, and that's that. I know what's going on. Selkirk thinks that if I write about what happened, I'll understand what

1

happened. Which makes no sense, if you stop and think about it, because if I don't understand what happened, how can I write about it?

Besides, I've done worse, *much* worse, and never written a word about it, and the fact that I never wrote about it had no effect, good or bad, so writing about it or not writing about it isn't going to prove a thing. I've got a good handle on who I am, if I say so myself. Compared with most twelve-year-olds, I mean. I'm not saying that I'm done growing up. I know I've got a long way to go. Sixth grade isn't the end of the line. My dad says that when he looks back to when he was a kid, he doesn't know whether to laugh or cry. I know there's going to be a Julian Twerski in the future who's going to look back the same way and maybe shake his head. (That last sentence should make you happy, Mr. Selkirk.) But when I look back *right now*, I'm just saying that what happened with Danley Dimmel isn't the worst thing I've done.

I'll give you a perfect example: Last year, Lonnie and I were out back in Ponzini doing nothing, just yakking it up. Now, I guess I should mention that Lonnie's my best friend. Except calling him my best friend doesn't tell how tight we are. My dad says that if Lonnie told me to jump, I'd ask, "How high?" He's being sarcastic, my dad, but he's right in a way. Because here's the thing: Lonnie wouldn't tell me to jump unless he had a good reason. So, yeah, I'd ask, "How high?" He'd ask me "How high?" too if I told him to jump. It doesn't mean a thing. I've known Lonnie since I was two and he was three, and some of the stuff that's gone on between the two of us he'd brain me if I ever wrote about, but I'm sure he'll be all right with me writing about the thing with the bird.

Oh, and I should also mention that Ponzini is what we call the lot behind the old apartment building on Parsons Boulevard where Victor Ponzini lives. Why we started calling it Ponzini is another story, and it doesn't matter for the bird story. So let's just say that Lonnie was the first to call it that, and it caught on with the rest of us. But it fits. It looks like a Ponzini kind of place.

If you want to picture it, picture a layer of brown dirt on a layer of gray cement about the size of a basketball court. It's got weeds growing out of it, and it's got broken glass around the edges, and it's got a half-dozen rusted-out wrecks that were once parked in the underground garage but got pushed out back when their owners skipped town. It's got rats, which should go without saying, but the rats only come out at night. In other words, it's foul and use-less, kind of like Victor Ponzini, who once squealed on Lonnie for cutting class. I mean, why is that Ponzini's business? The guy's a fifth grader and nothing but a tub of lard, but at least he knows it, which is about the only thing he's got going for himself.

So Lonnie and I were hanging out at the far end of Ponzini, just shooting the breeze, when I noticed that about a dozen pigeons had landed between two of the rusted-out wrecks. I nodded at the birds, and Lonnie glanced behind him, and I said, "What do you make of that?"

But in the time it took for the words to come out of my mouth, another half-dozen pigeons swooped down and landed. It was crazy—like a scene from that Alfred Hitchcock movie where a million birds get together and attack a town for no reason. There was no reason for them to show up in Ponzini either. There's not a thing for them to eat. I mean, it might make sense if someone had scattered bread crumbs for them. But there was nothing. It was as if one pigeon took it into its head that the far end of Ponzini would be a good place to rest for a minute, and then the entire air force joined in.

So the two of us were standing there watching, and in about a minute there were hundreds of pigeons crammed together between the two rusted-out wrecks, and the air was full of *prrriiiilllrrrps*—you know, that sound pigeons make. Their heads were bobbing up and down, ducking back and forth, and they were checking each other out. It was like a bird carnival. I'd never seen a thing like it.

That's when Lonnie turned to me and said, "Chuck a rock."

I just stared at him. It made no sense. "What do you mean?"

"I mean *chuck a rock*," he said.

"Why would I chuck a rock?"

He gave a slight laugh. "C'mon, Julian, chuck a rock."

"I'm not chucking a rock. *You* chuck a rock."

"Don't you want to see 'em take off at once?"

"I might hit one of 'em," I said.

"You're not going to hit one of 'em."

"How do you know?"

"Plus, even if you do, they're *pigeons*. They're filthy."

"I'm not chucking a rock—"

"C'mon," he said. "It'll be like a science experiment."

"How do you get that?" I asked.

"You think you'll hit one of 'em. I think you won't hit one of 'em. It's like you got a *hypothesis*, and I got a *hypothesis*, and now we're going to do a scientific experiment to see which one of us is right."

"You just want to see them take off at once."

"I never denied that," he said. "I'm just saying it's also science."

"Then why don't you do it?"

"First of all, because you've got a stronger arm than I do, so you can chuck the rock higher, which will give them more time to take off, and second of all, because it was my idea, and I want to watch 'em take off at once.

The sky's going to be full of pigeons, and I want to watch the thing from start to finish."

"You don't think I'm going to hit one of 'em?"

"There's *no way* you're going to hit one of 'em," Lonnie said. "It's like survival of the fittest. Use your brain, Julian. Do you think a pigeon makes it even one week in this neighborhood if he can't dodge a rock?"

He had me there. I'd seen hundreds of dead pigeons before. Pigeons that got run over by cars. Pigeons that got caught and chewed up by dogs and cats. Pigeons that got electrocuted on power lines. Pigeons that froze on tree branches and then dropped to the sidewalk still iced over. But not one of them, as far as I knew, ever got beaned by a rock.

I bent down and picked up a rock. It was gray with streaks of black running through it, maybe the size of a Reese's Cup, except kind of jagged and much heavier. The weight of it in my hand gave me second thoughts. I knew that if the rock hit one of the birds, it was going to hurt it bad. But then I thought that Lonnie was likely right, that the pigeons would see the rock coming and they'd all take off at once, and it would be something to see.

So I did it. I chucked the rock.

I knew it was a dumb thing to do, but I did it—which, now that I think about it, kind of makes my dad's point about Lonnie telling me to jump. Except it had gotten to where I *wanted* to chuck the rock, even though I knew it was dumb, because I wanted to see what would happen. Just to make sure, though, I screamed, "Heads up, birds!" real loud 'a second before I chucked it, and then I chucked it as high as I could, and that rock was no sooner in the air than the sky was full of birds, wave after wave of them, taking off before the rock even got to its highest point. There were so many of them in the air that it was hard to follow the upward flight of the rock because it was just another gray-and-black thing.

But you could follow it on the way down.

It was the only thing going in that direction, and that was when I realized that lots of birds were still going to be on the ground when it hit. They were crammed together too tight. There was no more room in the air for the stragglers to take off and no space on the ground for them to get out of the way.

It was maybe a second between the time I realized that and the time the rock hit, but that was one *long* second. My mind was racing forward, and I was grabbing at the air, clenching and unclenching my right hand, as if that would bring the rock back, as if I could undo how dumb I was for chucking it in the first place. Meanwhile, I was still hoping—no, I was *praying!*—that the rock would just clack down on the ground and nothing would happen.

But then the rock hit, and the sound wasn't a *clack*

but a soft *oof*, and I knew, from the sound, I'd hit a bird. I couldn't tell which one for another couple of seconds. That was how long it took for the rest of the birds to scatter and take off, and then there was only one left on the ground, flapping its wings like crazy but just going around in circles and raising a cloud of dust.

"Holy—!" Lonnie said.

"Oh no! Oh God . . . you said they'd get out of the way!"

"That was my *hypothesis*."

I ran over to the bird for a closer look. The poor thing was spinning around and around, getting nowhere. It wasn't bleeding, at least not that I could see. I thought for sure the rock had gashed it or split its skull wide open. But it looked kind of okay, except for the crazy way it was flapping its wings. Maybe it just needed to calm down for a minute and figure out it wasn't hurt too bad.

"C'mon," Lonnie called to me in a loud whisper. "Let's get out of here."

"No, wait!"

"Let's cheese it, Julian. It's over and done with."

"No!"

Lonnie came up behind me, and the two of us stared for about a minute as the pigeon began to tire itself out. It went from flapping around in a circle, to hopping side to side, to walking back and forth, to standing still with its head bobbing up and down. Then it stopped. It just sank to the ground and sat there.

"There, you see?" Lonnie said. "It's going to be just fine."

I took a step toward the pigeon. It stood up and walked a couple of bird steps away from me, then settled back down. I took another step, and so did the pigeon. "I don't think it can fly," I said.

"Sure it can. Watch. . . ."

Lonnie stepped in front of me and lurched at the pigeon. It fluttered its wings for a second but moved about six inches. Then he stamped his foot on the ground. This time the pigeon didn't react, except to turn its head away—as if it wasn't interested in what happened next.

Lonnie said, "That's one messed-up pigeon."

"What are we going to do?"

He shrugged. "Cheese it?"

"No, a cat's going to get it."

"Then there's only one thing left to do."

"What?"

"We've got to put it out of its misery."

"Kill it?"

"That's what you've got to do if it's dying."

"But we don't know for sure it's dying."

"Then let's get out of here!"

"But—"

"Julian, it's got to be one or the other."

Lonnie stepped past the pigeon and picked up the rock, the one I chucked, which was lying about a foot away. As soon as he picked it up, I closed my eyes real tight. I didn't want to see what he was about to do. But then, a second later, I felt him put the rock in my right hand. I opened my eyes and saw it there.

"Oh no—"

"You have to do it, Julian."

"Why do *I* have to do it?"

"Because you're the one who chucked the rock."

"But it was *your* idea."

"But I didn't chuck it."

"But it was your idea!"

"But I didn't chuck it!"

"C'mon, Lonnie—"

"Look, we can go back and forth forever. So I'm just going to tell you: *I'm not killing that bird.* So either you're going to do it, or we're going to leave the bird out here to die on its own. Those are the only two possibilities, okay?"

Say what you want about Lonnie, but he knows how to break things down. I didn't want the bird to die a long miserable death, but that's what was going to happen if I didn't do what was necessary. It's like Lonnie picked up the record needle and moved it to the end of the song. We both knew what I had to do. We just got there quicker than if we'd gone around in circles.

So I walked up to the bird until I was right over it— I didn't want to take a chance of missing with the rock or winging the poor thing and causing it to suffer even more. I had to go for the head. It had to be a kill shot. I thought about kneeling down next to the bird, but that meant I wouldn't be able to take a full windup. Instead I decided to straddle the pigeon, with one foot on either side of it, so that I could throw the rock straight down.

I reared back, but then, a split second before I fired the rock, I felt my eyes close. I came an inch from firing it blind—which was the last thing I wanted to do! So I shook my head, reared back again . . . and again I felt my eyes close. *C'mon!* I told myself. I reared back for a third time, and for a third time I felt my eyes close.

"What's the problem?" Lonnie said.

I took a deep breath. "It's no good."

"Just kill it."

"I keep closing my eyes."

"Well, then, don't close your eyes."

"Why didn't I think of that?" I said.

"You don't need to get sarcastic."

"I just want to get it over with."

"There's got to be a right way to do it." Lonnie started

glancing around, which is what he does when he's thinking real hard, and I knew, I just *knew*, he'd come up with an idea. Maybe ten seconds later he had one. He went running over to the far end of Ponzini and disappeared behind one of the rusted-out wrecks. Then, a few seconds later, he staggered back out.

He was lugging a concrete cinder block.

He shouted, "Hey, I could use a hand!"

So I ran over to him, and the two of us started lugging the cinder block back toward the pigeon. That cinder block weighed about a ton. I felt sadder and sadder with every step, thinking about what we were going to do with it, thinking about how helpless the pigeon was, thinking about how much pain I'd caused the poor thing so far, and about how much more it still had to go through. I mean, even if it was only for a split second, the pigeon was for sure going to feel the crush of the cinder block. But at least the end would be quick.

When we were about three steps from the pigeon, Lonnie stopped in his tracks and said, "You got it from here?"

I was huffing. "What do you mean?"

"It's a one-man operation."

"Lonnie!"

"Julian, you've *got* to do it."

"Why don't both of us do it?"

"Because if we do it together, we might not let go at the same time. Which means it might not fall straight down. That's the only way we might miss the bird."

I shook my head. "What you're saying is you won't do it, right?"

That cracked him up, despite the situation. He laughed and nodded.

I inhaled, then exhaled. "Fine, I've got it from here."

He let go of the cinder block, and I felt its full weight for the first time. I had to hold it tight to my body to keep from dropping it right there. It seemed to want to get out of my hands and fall to the ground, like I was keeping it from being where it was supposed to be.

With the cinder block hugged to my waist, I trudged the last three steps, and then I stepped over the pigeon so that the cinder block was centered above its skull, and I said a prayer for the pigeon—not out loud, just to myself—and I asked God to take mercy on it, and to take mercy on me for what I was about to do, and then at last I looked down, and the pigeon looked up at me, but it didn't make a move otherwise.

Except I couldn't do it.

I stepped back and dropped the cinder block a foot from the pigeon, which didn't flinch at the dull *thud* it made, the *thud* of concrete against concrete. Then I glanced back at Lonnie. He was standing with his hands on his hips, shaking his head.

"Now what?" he asked.

But then I had a thought. "I'll take it home."

He rolled his eyes. "You can't take that thing home."

"I'll just take care of it until it heals up."

"Your mom will go nuts. Pigeons are filthy birds."

He had a point, but I'd made up my mind. I knelt down next to the pigeon, and I slid my right hand underneath its body. The bird didn't like that one bit. It gave me a hard peck and fluttered out of reach. But I went after it. I knew the longer I chased it, the worse it would be. So I grabbed it with both hands before it could make another move. For a couple of seconds, nothing happened. I had it in my hands, and it didn't seem to mind. But then it began pecking the daylights out of me. My fingers. My palms. My wrists. I held on to it. I could feel how mad it was. It was like a wadded-up ball of anger, except with flapping wings and a pecking beak.

Finally, because I was afraid I would drop it, I held it to my chest and rolled it up inside my T-shirt. That calmed it right down. I could feel its heart beating against mine, and I glanced over at Lonnie, and he was rolling his eyes again like I'd gone nuts, which maybe I had, but I was going to do the right thing and heal up that pigeon.

Lonnie gave me a rap on the back for luck, but then he headed home, still shaking his head.

You can picture the expression on my mom's face when I came through the door with the pigeon. I know *I* was picturing it as I walked up the two flights of stairs, past the Dongs. The Dongs are the old Chinese couple who own the two-story house I live in. We rent out the top floor from them. They're good neighbors, quiet as can be, except Mrs. Dong cooks the foulest-smelling food you'd ever want to get your nose around. It doesn't taste bad—at least that's what my sister Amelia, who's five years older than I am, tells me. I wouldn't go near the stuff myself. But Amelia had dumplings and noodles with them once, and she lived to talk about it. Even so, when Mrs. Dong's got that stove going, my advice is hold your breath and run up the stairs as fast as you can.

I lucked out because Mrs. Dong wasn't cooking when I came back with the pigeon. But I was dreading the look my mom was going to give me. She was in the kitchen, and she heard me come through the door and called out her usual, "Supper's almost on the table, so wash up."

I could've gone straight to my room. But to get it over with, I walked into the kitchen, and I told her what I had rolled up in my shirt. That's when the look came. Her eyes narrowed down to slits, and her face seemed to go tired, like, *Oh, good grief!* But the thing was, once I started telling her what had happened, she softened up. She took a quick look at the pigeon, and she asked me if I was sure it couldn't fly, and I told her I was sure, and then she nodded and went into the hall closet and came out with a beat-up canvas suitcase. It was one she hadn't used in years. She told me I could keep the pigeon in the old suitcase until it healed up, and then I could throw out the suitcase. "Just make sure that bird doesn't wind up flying around the apartment," she said, then went back to the kitchen.

Sometimes when you brace yourself for a storm, you get a gentle breeze. The storm only comes when you're braced for nothing whatsoever.

I called out for Amelia, who was in her room at the far end of the apartment. I knew she'd lend a hand because she's soft for animals, so even if she had no interest in helping me out, she would want to save the pigeon. I was right. She dragged the suitcase into my room, and then she dragged in a week's worth of old newspapers my dad had piled up next to the couch. She tore up the papers and stuffed them in the suitcase so that the pigeon would have a nice feathery surface, and then I unrolled my shirt, and the pigeon plopped down and took a minute to collect itself—which is what you'd do too, if you'd been brained by a rock and then rolled up in a T-shirt.

But after a minute, the pigeon began to look around and seemed to realize it was all right.

Even though I didn't know if it was a he or a she, I decided to call the pigeon George Sauer after my favorite football player—the split end for the New York Jets. That annoyed Amelia. "If you name it, you're going to get attached," she said. "Then you're not going to want to set it free."

I told her she was wrong. I was only going to keep George Sauer until he healed up, and that was the end of it. "Once he can fly again, he's going out the window."

But of course she was dead right. I never should've named that bird. Never should have started to think about "it" as "him." You see, "it" isn't personal. But "him" . . . I mean, the minute I named the pigeon George Sauer, I began to notice how the name kind of fit him, how the shape of his head looked like a football helmet.

You've likely figured out the end of the story by now, so I won't beat around the bush. George Sauer never made it out of that suitcase. I fed him bread crumbs, but he got tired of that fast, and then I went to the pet store and bought him proper bird food, but he didn't take to that either. He couldn't right himself. He kept me up with *prrriiiilllrrrp* sounds the two nights he was in the suitcase, but by the third morning he was in a bad way. I could tell because when I reached into the suitcase, he didn't even bother to peck at me. So I picked him up, and I just held him for a minute. I stared into his eyes, as if he might forgive me for what I'd done to him. But I got nothing back. Not a thing. Just a look that seemed to be saying, *I'm a pigeon, for God's sake! I don't do stuff like forgive people!*

When George Sauer died that afternoon, I bawled my eyes out.

Me and Shakespeare

Selkirk got the biggest kick out of what I wrote so far. (Am I supposed to call you Mr. Selkirk whenever I write your name? Because, to be honest, that's not how kids talk about their teachers.) He says that writing is my thing, and that nothing's more important than doing your thing. So now he says that if I keep going with it, I can get out of the next few English assignments he's got lined up, and maybe even more after that. Which suits me just fine, if for no other reason than because I know what he's got lined up. Right there at the end, glaring up at me from the reading list he handed out after Christmas break, is *Julius Caesar*. I *hate* Shakespeare. I know that's hard for English teachers to hear, but it's the truth.

I didn't have a feeling about Shakespeare one way or

the other until two years ago, in fourth grade, when Mrs. Graber assigned each kid in the class a Shakespeare speech to learn by heart. We had to stand up in the front of the room and say our speech—which was bad enough, except it also meant we had to *listen* to the rest of the speeches. I got so sick of the stuff by the end that I could have vomited. It took up two full days in English class. What did I get out of it? The only thing I remember is the first line of my speech: "What a piece of work is a man!" That's it. I don't remember what came next, and I still don't know what in the world he's talking about.

So when I say I hate Shakespeare, I mean it. Lots of guys say they hate him, and what they mean is they hate the stuff he writes. But I don't only hate the stuff he writes. I hate *Shakespeare* for writing the stuff. I hate the *guy*, William Shakespeare. If I met him on the street, I'd just keep walking. Because you know, you just *know*, while he was writing the stuff he was writing, he was thinking how clever he was. He was sitting at his desk, writing the words, and he could've just said what he meant, but instead he prettied it up until it could mean everything or it could mean nothing or it could mean whatever the teacher says it means. That just drives me bananas. So if keeping this thing going gets me out of *Julius Caesar*, then count me in.

Heck, I'll write a whole book if it gets me out of Shakespeare.

Racing with Cars

Well, I guess the joke's on me. No sooner had I put that last sentence to paper, "Heck, I'll write a whole book if it gets me out of Shakespeare," than I ran smack into writer's block. That's what Selkirk called it. One minute I was writing like crazy, and then . . . *pffffft*. Nothing. I must have stared at those thirteen words for six hours—off and on, not six hours straight—and tried to come up with the next line, but it was as if my brain was spitting cotton. As if my skull was a movie theater and the audience was sitting there, waiting to watch the next movie, and I could hear the sound of crickets. It got to the point that I was about to throw in the towel, and I said so to Selkirk, but he told me about writer's block and said to keep going, even if

what I wrote didn't make sense, or even if it wasn't connected to what came before.

So . . .

Not to brag, but it's a well-known fact that I'm the
fastest kid in the sixth grade. Which means I'm the fastest kid in Public School 23, Queens, which only goes up
to the sixth grade. That's 997 students, and I can outrun
every last one of them. I once outran Mike the Bike—*on
his bike*! I raced him the entire length of Ponzini. It wasn't
even close. He said he eased up at the end because he was
afraid of crashing into the side of the building. I told him
I'd race him again, out on the street, and he said no. So
that was that.

What it reminded me of was that old John Henry
cartoon, you know, the steel-driving man versus the steel-
driving machine. Except I didn't drop dead at the end.
Yeah, I know. It's a stupid cartoon. It's also kind of preju-
diced against Negroes, if you look at it in a certain way.
Like when John Henry's mother says, "Pleezed to know
ya, son. I'ze your maw!" That's just not right, the way
it shows John Henry and his mom and his steel-driving
friends speaking such bad English. But as stupid as the
thing is, it makes me bawl like a baby. (It's not that I
cry a lot. The pigeon and the cartoon are just excep-
tional things, which is why I'm talking about them.) Even
though I know what's going to happen, even though I've

got the entire ending memorized, when that preacher says, "John Henry didn't die . . . no, he just stopped living in his mammy's shack, and he started living in the hearts of men forever and a day," that kills me every time. Even just writing about it chokes me up.

Anyway, it doesn't matter. My main point is that I've done worse things than the thing with Danley Dimmel, and one of those worse things was causing a car crash. I've never told this story before, not even to Lonnie. It happened a couple of years ago, so I figure enough time has passed. It also ties in with what I said before about outrunning Mike the Bike. That wasn't a big deal to me, or at least not as big a deal as the kids around here made it out to be, because I'd been outrunning *cars* for years. No lie.

Here's what I'd do: I'd wait on the corner of Parsons Boulevard and Thirty-Third Avenue. There's a traffic light there, so it was always a fair start. Then, when the light turned green and the car took off up Parsons, I'd take off on the sidewalk, and it was a race for the entire block to Thirty-Fourth Avenue.

Parsons is chewed up pretty good around there, scattered with potholes, so the driver would have to be nuts to step too hard on the gas. What I'm saying is, I know I can't beat a car on a level road. I'm not so stuck up as to think *that*. But with the potholes, I'd always pull ahead about two-thirds of the way up the block, and then we'd go neck and neck until I got to the corner at Thirty-Fourth Avenue, where there's no traffic light . . . and that's when I'd shoot out across Parsons, in front of the car. If the car had to slam its brakes, I counted that as a loss. But if it kept going without braking, I counted that as a win.

Except there was this one time I was going up against a brown Ford LTD. The driver was a Negro guy with a huge Afro haircut, which I noticed but didn't think too much about. I *should've* thought about it, though, because it meant he wasn't from the neighborhood and likely didn't know how chewed up the road was. So me and the LTD were going neck and neck the entire block, and I could hear him banging and skidding on the street next to me. When I shot across in front of him, he was so close that I could feel a gust of heat from his grill.

The car screeched. I knew I was safe because the sound was trailing off behind me. But when I glanced over my shoulder, I saw the LTD spinning out. I stopped and looked back. It was careening sideways toward the sidewalk on the west side of Parsons Boulevard. I watched it in disbelief. As the LTD jumped the curb, the guy had let go of the wheel, and he was holding his hands over his face. He'd given up trying to control the car. He was bracing for the crash. It came a second later. He hit the fire hydrant on the corner. The sound was just hideous, a sudden *pow*—like a paper bag popping, except much worse, much louder. I saw the guy's Afro jerking to the side, and then, a second later, he dropped out of sight.

I know it was a stupid thing to do, because I could've gotten in trouble, but I ran across the street to make sure he was all right. When I got to the car, he was slumped across the front seat, holding the side of his head and moaning.

"Hey," I called in to him. "Are you all right?"

He didn't answer. He just kept moaning.

"Hey . . . hey . . . ," I said.

"I'm all right," he mumbled, but he had a bad cut on his forehead. I could see the blood under his hand.

"You should get out of there," I told him.

"No, man, I'll be all right. Just let me be."

"But you're hurt."

"Let me be, man."

I wasn't listening to him. I started tugging on the driver's-side door. Except it was jammed shut. I couldn't budge it. The guy looked like he might have been able to kick the door out himself. He was young, maybe twenty years old, and the huge Afro made him look strong. Getting out of the car, though, seemed like the last thing on his mind. He was staring at his right hand, which was covered with blood, as if he was trying to figure out whose blood he was looking at.

That was when I heard the first siren. It was a couple

of blocks away, coming from the direction of Northern Boulevard.

"Oh, man," I heard him moan. He tried to straighten up, but it was no use.

"Just keep still," I told him. "The cops will get you out."

"Oh, *man!*"

"They'll be here in a minute," I said. "But I've got to go."

"Who are you?"

"I'm . . . I saw what happened."

"There was a kid who ran out in front of me."

"Sorry, I didn't see that. I just saw the crash."

"It was the kid's fault."

"I'm sorry . . . I'm so sorry."

He turned his head to face me. It took a lot of effort. I wanted to cheese it, but I felt like I should look him in the eye, like I owed it to him. There was blood gushing out of his forehead, clotting on his eyebrows and running down the bridge of his nose. As soon as he got a good look at me, he knew who I was. But he wasn't even mad. He muttered under his breath, "Oh, man!"

Then he just kind of smiled.

"I have to go," I said to him.

"You're a fast little dude."

"I'm so sorry. . . ."

"For a white boy, I mean."

"Really, I have to go."

"Do what you got to do."

As soon as he said that, I took off across Parsons Boulevard and ran as fast as I could up Thirty-Fourth Avenue. I wasn't a half block away when I heard the first police car pull up. But I didn't look back. It was like the story in the Bible, where the guy's wife looks back at Sodom and Gomorrah, and God turns her into a pillar of salt. That was how I felt. Like if I looked back, the cops were going to figure out what happened and come after me. Which I guess doesn't have much to do with the pillar of salt thing, now that I think about it, except it shows why you shouldn't look back.

But here's the kicker. It turned out *the car was stolen.* The guy came out of the accident all right, but he wound up in jail. I found out from the cops themselves. Two of them showed up in a squad car the next morning, asking around for witnesses. I was feeling real guilty and thinking about telling the truth, but then one of them mentioned the stolen car, and at that point I decided to lie through my teeth. Probably, I should've told the truth. But what was the point? He wasn't in trouble because he'd *crashed* the car. He was in trouble because he'd *stolen* the car. I had nothing to do with that. The crash was only the reason he got caught. Still, it's not as if I felt good about it.

That was the last time I raced a car up Parsons Boulevard.

Quentin's Eyebrows

You should've seen the look on Lonnie's face when I told him I was getting out of doing a book report on *Julius Caesar* by writing stories about myself. He didn't even believe me until I showed him what I had so far. He read the entire notebook, start to finish, and when he handed it back to me after school, he was real impressed. That made me feel good. Lonnie's not the kind of guy who blows smoke. He tells you the truth, whether it's going to hurt or not. Getting a thumbs-up from Lonnie meant more to me than getting an A on an English assignment, if that's what you decide to give me, Mr. Selkirk. (Hint, hint.)

There was only one thing I wrote that Lonnie didn't like. He said I made it sound as if the pigeon dying was his fault. Which it wasn't. I was the one who chucked the rock, so I'm the one who killed the pigeon. Lonnie only put the idea in my head.

Now that *that's* cleared up, I've got another story to tell. Lonnie's the one who reminded me of it when he read about the writer's block I had last week. He said I should write about the time Quick Quentin lost his eyebrows.

The thing about Quick Quentin is that he's just a great guy. That's an ironical nickname, by the way. He's a slow runner. Plus, he talks kind of slow. But he understands what he has to understand. He lives in the Hampshire House down by Union Street—which is also where Eric the Red and Howie Wartnose live. (That's not Howie's real last name, obviously. His real last name is Wurtzberg, but Lonnie called him Wartnose once and it stuck, even though he has a regular nose.)

That's our group: Lonnie, me, Quick Quentin, Eric the Red (because he has red hair), Howie Wartnose, and Shlomo Shlomo (because his mom always calls him twice for dinner). Lonnie's the one who thinks up nicknames for us. So far I don't have one, unless you count Julian Twerp. He called me that a couple of years ago after I intercepted a pass he threw during a football game. He was just frustrated. He didn't mean anything by it, and it never stuck. I'm sure it only came to him because "twerp" sounds like my last name, Twerski. But it hurt, kind of, since that's also what Amelia calls me when she gets in a bad mood. Twerp. Anyway, I'm sure Lonnie will come up with a good nickname for me sooner or later. That's what he does. It's one of the things that keeps us tight as a group. I mean, it's not like we're an official club. You don't get a membership card or a decoder ring. It's nothing like that. But it's hard for an outsider to join in because there's so much history. The time Quentin lost his eyebrows is a good example.

It happened on the playground out behind the Hampshire House. After Ponzini, that's where we hang out most often. We'd hang out there even more, but it's a regular playground with a swing set, a slide, and a couple of seesaws, so there's always moms and their kids hanging out too. I don't hold it against them. That's where I'd want to hang out if I were a kid. What I mean is, that's where I'd want to hang out if I were a *tyke*. My granny would always call me her "tyke" on account of I'm younger than Amelia. That made me a tyke, at least in her eyes. She was still calling me that when she passed away a couple of years ago. Except by then I was ten years old. What could I do? She was seventy-five years old. Even if I could change how she thought about things, what would be the point? She didn't mean it as an insult. Now she's dead and gone, and she's not going to come back to life, so it's a dead issue.

Well, the day Quentin lost his eyebrows was the fifth of July last year. I remember the exact date because it came right after the Fourth of July—which, I guess, is a stupid thing to say because the fifth of July always comes right after the Fourth of July. But the Fourth last year was a total washout. It rained from morning till night, so none of us had a chance to shoot off our fireworks, and on the fifth we were still walking around with pockets full of firecrackers and cherry bombs. Lonnie, I remember, had a couple of M-80s—which means he had, like, a half stick of dynamite in his jacket pocket.

The weather on the fifth wasn't much nicer than on the Fourth. It was overcast and real hot, which worked out well for us because the playground was muddy and the benches were wet. That kept the moms and their kids home. The entire back of the Hampshire House was ours. I remember it was Lonnie, me, Howie Wartnose, and Quick Quentin. Plus, Bernard and Beverly Segal were there. Bernard and Beverly are brother and sister. They hang out with us sometimes—mostly because Howie has been sweet on Beverly since the first time he laid eyes on her three years ago. He's never been the same since, and that was back in *third grade*. I mean, it just ruined him. There are times you can see his eyes go out of focus. That's what it's like. One second he's good old Howie, yakking it up, and then the next second, he notices Beverly Segal walking up the block, and he's like a zombie, shuffling his feet back and forth, staring down at the sidewalk or straight ahead at nothing. You want to tell him to let it go. Because of him, the rest of us have to put up not only with Beverly—who's all right by herself—but also with Bernard, who's still in fourth grade and almost as big a waste of human ingredients as Victor Ponzini.

So it was maybe eight o'clock, not quite dusk, but without the sun it felt later, and the six of us were out behind the Hampshire House, when Lonnie came up with the idea of lighting our leftovers. Right off, Howie whipped out about ten sheets of firecrackers. That caught Beverly's eye—it was probably more firecrackers than she'd ever seen in her life. She asked if she could set one off, meaning one single firecracker, but of course Howie melted to gooey cheese at the sound of her voice, so he handed her an entire sheet. Twenty-four firecrackers. She just stared at them. She didn't have a match, so there was no way to set them off. But she half smiled at Howie, and he went from gooey cheese to buttermilk in about five seconds, and mumbled, "You're welcome."

The only problem was that Beverly still hadn't thanked him. So she had to spit out a late thank-you because she thought he was being sarcastic and telling her off, like, *Hey, weren't you supposed to thank me?* Then Howie came back with something real intelligent, like, "Oh, no . . . no, no . . . I, er, I didn't . . . I didn't mean, er . . . no . . ."

It was just sad.

That was when Lonnie pulled out a book of matches, maybe because he couldn't stand watching Howie make a fool of himself for another second. So we started setting off our firecrackers. We set them off an entire sheet at a time, with the joint fuse that comes in the package, because it wasn't like Lonnie had a million matches. First Howie did a couple of sheets, then Quentin, then me.

When Beverly tried, her hand kept shaking, and she couldn't get the fuse lit—it's harder to light up the joint fuse than to do it one firecracker at a time. It was comical to watch, but after half a minute Lonnie got tired of it. "Here," he said. He grabbed her hand and steadied it, and she managed to set off her sheet. She was dancing around the thing, whooping like an Indian as it was going off, and Howie was just kind of looking at her, *gazing* at her, if you know what I mean, knowing that his firecrackers got her excited—but also, you could see it in his eyes, ticked off that Lonnie had grabbed her by the hand.

After a couple more minutes, we were down to our last three matches. Which was a problem because Quentin still had a cherry bomb, Lonnie still had both M-80s, and Howie still had three more sheets of firecrackers.

That was when Lonnie had one of his brainstorms. He looked around and noticed a paper cup on the ground under one of the benches and told Bernard to grab it for him.

Bernard was glad to do it. I think he was glad Lonnie remembered he was still standing there, off to the side, twiddling his thumbs. So he snatched the cup and handed it to Lonnie, who used the bottom of Bernard's T-shirt to clean out the mud that was caked inside. Then Lonnie wedged the cup into the wet ground, and he broke open his M-80s and dumped the powder into the cup. Quentin caught on to the plan, and he cracked open his cherry bomb and did the same thing. Howie came forward too and started breaking open his last three sheets of firecrackers—except he had to do it one firecracker at a time. Quentin knelt down and lent him a hand, and the rest of us were getting more and more excited by what was about to happen. I mean, this thing was going to be a *bomb* when it went off.

Meanwhile, Bernard started whining that he still hadn't set off even one firecracker. He must have figured we owed him that much because Lonnie used his shirt to clean out the cup. To shut him up, Howie handed him one of his last firecrackers—the cup was filled to the rim with powder now anyway. Lonnie handed Bernard the matchbook, but he told him he could only use one match. Because, again, we only had three matches left.

Right off, I knew Bernard wasn't going to be able to light the firecracker with just one match. No way. Guys like Bernard Segal can never do that kind of stuff. That's just how the world works. So while Quentin and Howie were patting down the powder in the cup, I could hear Bernard behind me . . . *scratch, scratch, scratch.*

Finally, I'd had enough. I stood up and said, "Here, let me strike it for you."

"No!" he yelled. "I want to do it!"

"You can still light the thing. I'll just strike the match."

"No!" Bernard's eyes were wide, and he looked like he was about to bawl. He was shaking his head, his mop of ratty yellow hair going back and forth.

I didn't want to make the kid bawl, so I took a couple of steps back. But that didn't calm him down. He was even more frantic to strike the match, and he kept scratching it and scratching it against the matchbook. It was no good. He wasn't even close to getting a spark. Plus, the match was getting bent up and useless. So of course Bernard kept gripping it higher and higher, until he was holding it almost by the match head. Which meant that if he ever did spark it up, he was going to burn himself.

Sure enough, just as I was thinking that it would serve

him right, the match head sparked up. It flamed right between Bernard's thumb and forefinger, and he yelped and got rid of it. And I was watching the flaming match head shoot through the air. It didn't even occur to me to look where it was going.

Right for the paper cup.

Howie noticed it out of the corner of his eye, and he dove out of the way. But poor Quentin, he was still patting down the powder to a perfect flat surface inside the cup. He had no idea what was flying in his direction.

The match head landed smack in the middle of the cup just as Quentin started to lean back and admire his handiwork. There was a split second—not even a split second, like half a split second—where nothing happened. Quentin was smiling at the thing, and the match head was glowing against the black surface of the powder, and it was real and unreal at the same time.

But then, a split second later, the fireball came. It wasn't loud, not a *bang* or a *pop*, just kind of a *whoosh*. Quentin's face lit up. His entire head was surrounded by flames and smoke. It was like something you'd see in a comic book. You know, like *The Adventures of the Human Fireball*. Again, it was only for a split second. Not enough time to realize what was going on, or to think about the consequences—like maybe Quentin was going to be dead once the smoke cleared.

His hands went up to his face, and he started rolling around on the ground. Right off, we scrambled over to him, all of us, even Bernard, but Quentin wouldn't take his hands away to let us look at him. He was just rolling from side to side, cussing and moaning. To be honest, I was kind of relieved that he was reacting like that. It meant that his head hadn't gotten blown off and that his arms and legs still worked and that he could still get words out of his mouth.

It took maybe a minute before Lonnie could pry Quentin's hands away from his face. As soon as he did, the rest of us took a step forward. I didn't know what I was about to see—whether he was going to have a monster face with gooey bubbling flesh or what. I held my breath, then exhaled when I could still recognize Quentin. He was lying still now, with his hands at his sides. His face looked like someone took a handful of grease and dirt and smeared it from the peak of his forehead to the tip of his chin. Even his ears were smeared over. But at least he was still recognizable.

"Can you open your eyes?" Lonnie asked him.

"No," Quentin said, just loud enough for us to hear.

"Try to."

"I can't."

"Do you mean you can't because you're blind?"

"I can't do it!"

"That's all right," Lonnie said, calm as can be.

Quentin calmed down too. "What happened?"

Lonnie ignored him. "How do your eyes feel?"

"I don't know. Sticky."

"Sticky how? Your eyeballs or your eyelids?"

"I don't know."

"You need to open your eyes."

"I can't, Lonnie."

"If you can't, I'll do it for you."

"No!"

"Quentin, I'm going to open your eyes. You can help me or not, but I'm going to do it."

Lonnie sounded so sure of himself that Quentin didn't answer. But he didn't resist either. He lay still with his hands at his sides. Lonnie licked the tip of his thumb and forefinger, then reached toward Quentin's face. He was real gentle—as gentle as I'd ever seen him—as he cleared the gunk from Quentin's eyelids.

"Hey, are you still all right?" Lonnie asked.

"Yeah."

"Me doing that, does it hurt?"

"Nah." Quentin half smiled.

"You think you can open them yourself now?"

"Maybe."

His eyelids fluttered for a second, then came open.

"Do you see me, Quent?"

He smiled fuller this time. "Yeah."

"How many fingers do I have up?"

"None."

"Yeah," Lonnie said, "it was a trick question."

"I think maybe I'm okay," Quentin said.

I could've kissed him when he said that. No, honestly, I could've knelt down next to him and kissed him on both cheeks. Except I knew he *wasn't* okay. The smell of singed hair was hovering all around us, and I could see filthy clumps of hair high on Quentin's forehead that were no longer connected to his scalp.

"We've got to get you cleaned up," Lonnie said.

"Yeah."

"Can you sit up?"

"I think so, yeah."

With that, Quentin tucked his legs in and pushed himself up onto his elbows. He sat in that position for maybe half a minute, blinking his eyes and licking his lips. He looked woozy. You'd be woozy too if an atom bomb went off in your face. You'd likely be pretty mad too, asking how it happened, who did what. But not Quentin. That's not his way.

Lonnie asked, "How do you feel?"

"Let me just sit here for a while," he mumbled.

Then Lonnie looked up at me. "We need a bar of soap and, like, ten paper towels. Half of 'em wet. How fast can you get that?"

I didn't even answer him. I just took off and ran like crazy . . . out of the playground, then up the block in the direction of my house. The sidewalk was deserted, so I got up to a good cruising speed. I had to dodge old Mrs. Dong as I yanked open the front door to my house and hurtled up the stairs. She started laughing and jabbering at me in Chinese. She must've thought I was out of my mind. The only thing that slowed me down was getting the key out of my back pocket and fitting it into the lock. But a second later I was inside.

"Is that you, Julian?" came my mom's voice from the bedroom.

"I need paper towels," I called back.

"What for?"

"I just need 'em."

She started to laugh too. "All right, take as many as you want."

I spun that roll of towels round and round. I didn't even bother to count the sheets. I tore off what I needed and ran half of them under warm water. I was gasping for air at that point, but wetting the towels slowed me down enough to catch my breath. When I was done, I snatched the bar of Ivory soap next to the sink and tucked it into my pocket.

My mom called out, "Is everything all right?"

I didn't answer her. I had what I needed.

"Julian? Are you still there?"

"I took the soap too, Mom."

"What's going on?"

But by then I was back out the door, back down the stairs, back outside, and I was making a beeline for the back of the Hampshire House. I had the damp end of the strip of paper towels hugged close to my body, the dry end streaming out behind me like the tail of a comet. I felt like a comet too—that's how fast I was going. I remember a car honking at me just for the heck of it. Like, *Go, man, go!* That was how it sounded to me at the time. But looking back, it could have been sarcastic too. Like, *Slow down, you moron!* I guess you hear what you want to hear.

The first thing I saw when I turned into the playground was Quentin sitting on one of the wooden benches. That was a good sign, even though it meant his pants were getting soaked in the leftover rainwater—like he didn't have enough problems. He still looked wobbly and out of it. His shoulders were slouched forward, but at least he was sitting up on his own. Lonnie and Howie were standing in front of him, telling him he was all right. Beverly and

Bernard had taken off, which was just as well. Without Beverly around, Howie would be in his right mind.

Lonnie tore off a couple of the wet paper towels and began to wipe Quentin's face. He started with his cheeks and chin, then did the bridge of his nose. You should have seen the crud that came off! He did Quentin's forehead next. He tried to be gentle about it, but tufts of hair fell off. Even if he wiped underneath them, the tufts stuck to the paper towel, or else they came loose and drifted to the ground. If Quentin noticed, he didn't react.

Lonnie told him, "Now close your eyes, Quent."

Quentin closed his eyes.

Lonnie took the rest of the paper towels, first the damp ones and then the dry ones, and went to work on Quentin's eyes. He used every last one I brought because, you could tell, he didn't want to put pressure on the eyelids. He was just dabbing, not rubbing. But after a couple of passes, Quentin's eyebrows were starting to go. There was nothing Lonnie could do. His eyebrows were gone whether Lonnie stopped wiping or not. By the time Quentin's face was clean, not a hair of either eyebrow was left. It was creepy to look at. Not that he was messed up or deformed. He just looked stunned. Like he was stuck in a constant state of *Yikes!*

Quentin noticed the hairs on the paper towel and figured out what had happened. He felt for his eyebrows, and then—I swear!—he started to crack up. It was the craziest laugh ever. Maybe he was so relieved to be alive that losing his eyebrows seemed like a minor thing. Whatever the reason, the fact that he was cracking up cracked up Lonnie and Howie and me, and for a minute the four of us were in hysterics. It was as if we were cracking up at ourselves, at the fact that we were cracking up.

But then Howie brought us back to reality. "Your mom's going to *kill* you."

That simmered us down right away.

Quentin looked up at Lonnie. You could see the fear in his eyes maybe for the first time. "What are we going to do?"

Lonnie gave it a couple of seconds of thought. Then he turned to me. "Is Amelia home?"

"I don't know," I said.

"She's got makeup, right?"

"Sure she does," I said. "Lots of it. It takes up an entire shelf in the bathroom—"

"Do you know what eyeliner is?"

That's when it hit me. "Yeah, I do."

So I took off like I did before. I was still out of breath from the first run . . . but it was a case where you do what you have to do. My mom didn't even ask me what I was doing rushing through the house like a maniac. She must have heard me run into the bathroom and figured she knew what I was doing. (I did pee, actually.) Then I ran back out without a word.

About a minute later, I was back in the playground with Amelia's eyeliner. Howie was gone when I got there—now it was just Lonnie, Quentin, and me. It took Lonnie at least ten minutes to draw two new eyebrows for Quentin. He did a real good job too. It was a talent I didn't know he had. I guess *he* didn't know he had it either because, after he was done, the two of us were kind of shocked at how good Quentin's new eyebrows looked. Sure, if you were looking right in his face, staring him down, you'd figure out that his eyebrows were fake. But if you were just glancing at him, you wouldn't notice.

That's what I was thinking when Howie came running back into the playground. He was holding a can of Glade air freshener, which he gave to Lonnie. It took me about a second to realize why.

"Hey, are you sure that's a good idea?" I asked him.

Quentin caught sight of the can. "What's that for?"

Lonnie got right to the point. "You reek, Quent."

"I do?"

"You reek of burnt hair."

"I can't smell it." Quentin turned to me. "Do I?"

"Yeah, you do," I answered. "But I'm not sure—"

Lonnie glared at me. "You have a better idea?"

I thought it over. "What if we take him back to your house and wash his hair?"

"If we do that, more hair's going to fall out. It needs time to settle back in."

That seemed like bad logic, so I turned to Quentin. "You all right with this?"

He shrugged. "Well, I can't go home if I reek of burnt hair."

"If you go home reeking of burnt hair, there's a one-hundred-percent chance you're dead," Lonnie said. "If you go home reeking of Glade, there's a ninety-nine percent chance you're dead. You can make up your own mind, Quent, but if it's me, I'm going to choose the ninety-nine percent."

Once Lonnie laid it out like that, there *was* no choice.

Quentin covered his eyes and smiled. "You may fire when ready."

As soon as he heard that, Lonnie let him have it. He emptied the entire can on him. There was a cloud of the stuff hanging in the air around Quentin's head. It filled our noses, and I thought for a minute Lonnie's idea might work, but as soon as the cloud began to clear, the smell of burnt hair came back. It was just underneath the smell of Glade.

Quentin looked hopeful, but in the end we had to tell

him that the smell was back, that he still reeked. Plus, now his hair was matted down with a sheen of air freshener. As soon as he washed it, or even ran a comb through it, you could tell that patches were going to come out. Which meant that his mom was going to know. About his hair. About his eyebrows.

He was dead.

I said I'd walk him home, and Howie said he would too. Lonnie didn't see the point of it, but in the end, he said he'd come along if Quentin thought it would make a difference. But Quentin shook his head. What was the point?

He wasn't going to rat us out.

It took six weeks for Quentin's eyebrows to grow back. He had to get a crew cut to even out his hair. But the worst of it was that his dad took the stereo out of his room. Quentin *loves* music. He listened to the Beatles' *White Album* as he went to sleep. When I heard what his dad did, I wanted to knock on their door and tell him that it wasn't Quentin's fault, that if Bernard Segal hadn't been messing around with that match, nothing bad would've happened. But I knew he wasn't going to believe me.

I wouldn't have believed me if I hadn't been there to see it happen.

Messing with Mr. Caricone

I'm guessing you know by now, Mr. Selkirk, that I got thrown out of Mr. Loeb's social studies class last week. I'm guessing that's the kind of thing teachers talk about in the teachers' lounge, especially since it came after the suspension in January. But this is nothing like what happened with Danley Dimmel. The thing in Mr. Loeb's class was just a joke I should have kept to myself. No big deal. So you guys can go back to talking about the usual stuff, like whether to erase the blackboard from top to bottom, or from side to side, or around and around in a mishmash.

I'm just kidding, of course. I know teachers have regular lives when you're not in school. As a matter of fact, my aunt Tillie used to be a teacher. Now she's a bookkeeper, but she once taught an art class at Queens College. She's real serious about art—the walls of our house are covered with paintings she did. She's always taking Amelia to museums, and the two of them come home yakking it up about Rembrandt or Michelangelo. I think Amelia's going to follow in her footsteps. She doesn't paint yet, but she draws in a huge sketch pad. She's getting good too. No matter what she draws, it always looks like the thing. Plus, she's always borrowing art books from the library. My mom says she's caught the art bug.

The only reason I mention my aunt Tillie is so you know I've got nothing against teachers. That's why I feel so lousy about what happened in social studies class. Lots of kids goof on teachers—how they're hard cases and how they've got nothing else to do so they make you work, work, work because it fills the hole in their lives. But I know that teachers are just human beings. Some are downright decent. They make you work hard, but they also let you get creative every now and then. (Which is the reason you're reading these words, if you stop and think about it, Mr. Selkirk.) My main point is that I wouldn't disrespect a teacher on purpose.

That goes double for Mr. Loeb. He's a decent guy, and a decent teacher, and he's always been decent to me. Plus, he's a josher, which I like. He'll go back and forth with you. Like how he calls Tedd Alford "Mr. Dalford." As if one of the d's in Tedd's first name is supposed to go at the start of his last name. Like it's a mistake his parents made on the birth certificate. That sounds kind of cruel written out like that, but Mr. Loeb also teases himself. He calls himself The Ear. Like in Ear Loeb . . . earlobe. Get it? If he sees you yawning in his class, he'll lower his voice and call you out right then and there: "Mr. Twerski, The Ear has got his eye on you." That cracks me up every time.

But in a sense, that's what got me in trouble, because social studies is such a joshing kind of class that sometimes it's hard to remember you're in school and you have to get down to business. Not that I blame Mr. Loeb for what happened. It was totally my fault. I had it coming. He always said we could josh around with him but not with Mr. Caricone, the student teacher who teaches us on Fridays. I knew what the rules were, but I got carried away.

So here's what happened with Mr. Caricone. It started, I guess, a couple of weeks ago, when he taught us about India. I liked the stuff about the caste system—how Indian society is divided up into classes of people with some in the upper class and some in the lower class and the rest in between. You know, the Brahmins versus the untouchables. I like that kind of stuff.

But it wasn't just the caste system. We got real deep into India. I think it's maybe Mr. Caricone's favorite thing to teach about. We learned how there are, like, a hundred different religions in India, and how Indians are always fighting over their religious beliefs. Let me tell you, that made me glad to be an American. Then we talked about overpopulation, and it just amazed the heck out of me how many Indians live in India. It's got, like, three times the population of the United States. I don't know how they can live squeezed together like that. Maybe that's why they're always fighting with each other. They need more elbow room. But the thing Mr. Caricone stressed is that no one even knows what the real population of India is. Lots of Indians live in tents or in refrigerator boxes or even in drainage pipes, so they don't have an address, or else they don't know how to write their names, or else they don't trust the government, so the census takers go from town to town and make an educated guess about how many people live there. It's very inexact.

So that was the week before last. Now remember that Mr. Loeb is real protective of Mr. Caricone—because he's a new teacher, I mean. He doesn't want us to razz him. Which I never meant to do. Except then Mr. Caricone began last week's class with the question "Does anyone remember how the government takes the census in India?"

I called out, "One little, two little, three little Indians!"

The entire class cracked up. It was just a tidal wave of laughter.

Look, it's not as if I rehearsed the joke beforehand. It just came to me when Mr. Caricone asked that question, and I said it out loud, and the entire class cracked up, and Mr. Caricone's face went red. I thought for a second he was going to break down and bawl his eyes out. He didn't, of course. He kept going. But he was shaken up. It was just a joke, but it shook him up. What I said was wrong, and as soon as I said it, I *knew* it was wrong, but I couldn't take it back.

So on Monday morning, Mr. Loeb kicked me out of social studies class. He made me drag my desk out into the hall, outside the classroom door, and take notes from there. It was shameful. Principal Chapnick walked past at one point, and she asked me what I was doing out in the hall, and I had to tell her. The look she got on her face—since she was the one who suspended me after the thing with Danley Dimmel—felt like it burned a hole right through me.

The worst of it, though, was knowing what I did to Mr. Caricone. I mean, I shook him up bad. You could hear it in his voice for the rest of the class, like a rattle underneath the words. I told Lonnie how low I felt afterward, and he told me I was nuts to give it a second thought. He said either Caricone would shrug it off, so there was no harm done, or else it would ruin him as a teacher, so he didn't belong in front of a classroom in the first place. That's classic Lonnie, putting things in a logical perspective. But I still felt low about it.

February 13, 1969

The Love Letter

As if I don't get enough homework from school, now I've got to write a love letter for Lonnie. Maybe it's because Valentine's Day is around the corner, or maybe it's just how my luck is running, but for whatever reason, he's got it bad—not quite as bad as Howie Wartnose has got it for Beverly Segal, but bad enough—for a girl named Jillian Rifkin, who moved here a couple of months ago from somewhere like Ohio. She lives clear across the school district, at the west edge of Bayside. If she'd moved another block east, she would've wound up going to P.S. 22, and I wouldn't be stuck writing a love letter for Lonnie.

Still, it's not as though Lonnie doesn't have good taste. I mean, I get it. Jillian is real gorgeous. She's got dark brown hair that goes straight down to her waist, big brown eyes, and a perfect dot of a nose. Plus, she's got the whitest teeth I've ever seen. She must brush her teeth about ten times a day. So I can't blame Lonnie for feeling how he feels. I blame literature.

Yeah, I know, Mr. Selkirk. That's not what you want to hear, given how you're always telling us how novels and poems and plays broaden our horizons. I don't doubt they do. But what if they also make us mental? What I mean is, maybe Lonnie would've liked Jillian even if he hadn't been studying *Cyrano de Bergerac,* but there's no way he would've asked me to write a love letter for him if not for the part where Cyrano tells the other guy the words to say to get Roxane to love him. It's just a totally mental plan. Not to mention that it doesn't even work for Cyrano. I read the book last year. Roxane winds up marrying that other guy, even though Cyrano loves her, and then good old Cyrano gets hit by a log dropped from a window.

I told Lonnie it was a totally mental plan. I used those exact words. We were walking home from school, and I told him the plan had no chance of working, and I didn't want to be part of it.

"C'mon," he said. "What did I ever ask you to do for me except this?"

"That's not the point. I'd do it for you if I thought it would work—"

"It *will* work," he said.

"How will it work?"

He stopped in his tracks and faced me. He tried to come up with an answer. The air was cold enough to see his breath as he thought about it, but no words came out. Then at last he said, "It just will. It has to."

"Then why don't you write it yourself?"

I realized as soon as I said it that that was a mean thing to say to him. Lonnie's always been self-conscious about his writing, about grammar and spelling and such. I wanted to take it back, except the words were out of my mouth. But Lonnie let it go. He got a real wounded look in his eyes, but he let it go. He just said, "C'mon, Julian! I *need* you!"

"Why don't you just talk to her?"

"And say what?"

"I don't know. Say your piece."

"What does that even mean?"

I had to think about it. "I guess it means say whatever comes to you."

"What if nothing comes to me?"

"Sooner or later, no matter what, you're going to have to talk to her."

"But if she already likes me by then . . ."

He let the thought trail off. I knew where he was going with it.

"Let's say I write the letter for you. How would we get it to her? Do you know her address?"

"You could just pass it to her—"

"Oh, no!"

"C'mon, I don't know anyone else in any of her classes."

"Lonnie, it's a totally mental plan—"

"Maybe if I was in the *gifted* class . . ."

"C'mon, Lonnie. That's not fair."

"But you *are* in the gifted class."

"That's not my fault," I said.

"No one said it was your fault. But it means you're in a certain position."

"What kind of position?"

"You have responsibilities," he said.

"How do you get that?"

"Not everyone writes as good as you."

"So what?"

"Look, if you needed to drag a couch down the street, you'd come to me, right?"

"I guess so, but—"

"Why would you come to me?"

"Because you're my friend."

"And?"

I thought it over. "Because you're stronger than I am."

"Exactly!"

"But—"

"You're a better writer than I am," he answered. "I'm coming to you because I need to get a letter written. The same way you'd come to me to get a couch dragged down the street."

"But I've never asked you to drag a couch down the street," I said. "Plus, why would anyone want to drag a couch down the street in the first place? It doesn't make sense."

"That's beside the point," he said.

"How could that be beside the point? That *is* the point!"

"No, the point is that you're my best friend—or at least, I thought you were. The point is that writing a letter or dragging a couch are the kinds of things best friends do for each other."

"But best friends also tell each other the truth."

"True," he said.

"So if I know it's not going to work—"

"Then let me find out for myself. Otherwise, it'll always be gnawing at me."

You know how people talk about the end of the world, how there will be signs like the stars lining up a certain way, and the seas giving up their dead, and lambs lying down with lions? For me, a sure sign of the end of the world will be when I can win an argument with Lonnie.

So the long and short of it is that I wound up saying

I'd write the love letter for him, even though the thing has no chance of working, and even though he'll likely blame me when it doesn't. Plus, even if it does work—which, if you think about it, would be another sign of the end of the world—that would only mean Lonnie would wind up doing stuff with Jillian instead of with the guys on the block. So it's a lose-lose situation, as far as I'm concerned.

But I'll give it my best shot. Because it's Lonnie.

The first thing I did was borrow a poetry book from the school library. I thought about borrowing one of Amelia's. She's got a stack of poetry books in her room. Not even for school. She just reads them on her own. But I knew if I asked to borrow one of her books, she'd want to know why. The point is, girls *love* poetry. I don't get it, to tell the truth. Then again, I'm not a girl. On the other hand, Jillian *is* a girl. So I figured, if you're going to write a love letter to a girl, studying up on a book of poems seemed like a good place to start.

But the thing was, once I got going, the poems weren't half bad. Maybe because I was reading them for Lonnie's sake instead of for an assignment, which meant I could just relax and take them in. If one of them bored me, I could just turn the page and not worry about getting quizzed on it. But the real ironical thing is that I even read a couple of poems by *Shakespeare*.

The first one was decent enough. It starts off, "Shall I

compare thee to a summer's day?" I like that. It says what it says. Except for "thee." But if that's how people said "you" back in Shakespeare's time, then maybe he couldn't help himself. The rest of it's like that too. It gets egotistical at the end, when he says that the girl will live forever because of the poem. But you know what? He was right. I just read the poem, and I wound up thinking about the girl, so in a way the girl *is* still alive. She did live forever. I don't know if that's what he meant, but whatever he meant, it's a decent poem. I was glad I read it.

The second Shakespeare poem wasn't as good. It kind of made me mad at him again. It's the one that starts out, "Let me not to the marriage of true minds admit impediments." First off, I had to look up about half the words. Second, he rhymes "love" with "remove." I mean, either you're writing a rhyming poem or you're not writing a rhyming poem. You don't get half credit just because the two words are spelled alike.

But you know what poem stuck out? "My True Love Hath My Heart" by Sir Philip Sidney. I'd never heard of the guy before, and he's as old as Shakespeare, but he's not as complicated or egotistical. The poem was only fourteen lines long . . . and I got it the first time through. That's how a poem should work. It's about a guy and a girl who trade hearts with one another, and how each one takes care of the other one's heart, and how both hearts ache with love, and how the pain brings them closer together. That's the entire poem in a nutshell. I read the poem over and over until I could almost recite it with my eyes closed:

> My true-love hath my heart and I have his,
> By just exchange one for the other given:
> I hold his dear, and mine he cannot miss;
> There never was a bargain better driven.
> His heart in me keeps me and him in one;
> My heart in him his thoughts and senses guides:
> He loves my heart, for once it was his own;
> I cherish his because in me it bides.
> His heart his wound received from my sight;
> My heart was wounded with his wounded heart;
> For as from me on him his hurt did light,
> So still, methought, in me his hurt did smart:
> Both equal hurt, in this change sought our bliss,
> My true love hath my heart and I have his.

It's kind of humorous, the way it sounds, but also romantic, and it made me think about love and life, which proves you don't need to get so flowery and so complicated to get your message across.

So, to come to the point, after a couple of hours of flipping through the poetry book and rolling poems around

and around in my head, I got real inspired and sat down
to write Lonnie's love letter to Jillian.

Here's what I came up with:

Dear Jillian,

　　Lots of guys only give away their heart
if they know they're going to get a heart
in return, so it evens out. But I think giving
away your heart means more when you don't
know what's going to happen, when you might
get nothing back. You might have to walk
around afterward with a big hole where
your heart used to be, knowing a girl has
your heart and you'll never have hers. But
it doesn't matter. Because what good is a
heart if you keep it to yourself? So instead
of giving you a card this Valentine's Day,
I wanted you to have my heart. Not because
I expect your heart in return. But just
because I know my heart will be happy if you
keep it next to yours for a little while.

Sincerely,
Your secret admirer

After I wrote it down, I read it over a couple of times.
Then I typed it up. I figured I had to type it up because

girls like to save love letters. Which meant, down the line, Jillian would be able to compare my handwriting to Lonnie's. I mean, if it ever came to that. Which I still highly doubted.

The last step was to show it to Lonnie. No way was I going to pass the letter to Jillian until he'd given me the go-ahead.

He started to nod as soon as he read the first line, and by the end he had a big grin on his face. He said it was as if I'd read his mind. But he also wanted me to put in something about her being cool. He wanted me to use the word "cool." I told him "cool" didn't go with the rest of the letter. Lonnie thought about it some more, and then he said that, well, of course I knew best because I was in the *gifted* class, which he said in a sarcastic way. So in the end I changed the ending to "because I know you're real cool, and my heart will be happy if you keep it next to yours for a little while"—which meant I had to retype the letter. But I figured he should have the final say-so.

It was *his* letter.

Getting the letter to Jillian was more awkward than I thought it would be. My plan was to get it over with as fast as possible. I was torn between saying "Somebody asked me to give this to you" and "Here, this is for you." I figured I'd go with whichever felt right at the moment. I waited until right after English period so I knew she'd be in a reading mood, and then I walked up to her with the letter behind my back.

Jillian looked at me in a strange way, and her face went red even before I started to talk, and that made me feel strange, doing what I was doing. Suddenly, neither of the sentences I'd rehearsed felt right. There was a long pause with the two of us just standing there outside the door of the classroom. The hall was full of kids rushing off to the cafeteria for lunch. But it was like time stopped as I struggled to talk. I mean, it was real uncomfortable. I tried to figure out a gradual way to lead up to slipping her the letter, but nothing came to me. She was looking me right in the eye, and my mind was a total blank.

Then she said, "Why don't you ever raise your hand in class?"

That was just such a weird question. It threw me. "I don't know."

She smiled. "I *always* raise my hand when I know the answer."

"So do I."

"Tell the truth!"

"Maybe I don't feel like answering the question," I said.

"It's nothing to be ashamed of."

I squinted at her. "What are you talking about?"

"Knowing the answer. It's nothing to be ashamed of."

"Why would I be ashamed of it?"

"I don't know. Why *would* you?"

"I'm not ashamed of knowing the answer. I just don't always like to show it off."

"But if you *know*—"

"If I know, then I know. And I know I know. That's enough."

"If I know the answer, I want *everyone* to know I know."

"Why?" I asked, not even thinking about the letter anymore.

"Just because," she said.

"That's not even an answer," I said, which might have come off as annoyed. If it did, it's because I was. I still hadn't given her the letter, and I'd gotten sucked into a conversation that made no sense.

"But it's the truth. I always tell the truth."

"No one *always* tells the truth."

"I do . . . except when I don't."

She smiled at me again. I thought she meant it as a joke, but I wasn't sure, so I didn't smile back at her. Then came about three seconds in which nothing happened. I felt the letter in my left hand, slightly behind my back, and began to bring it forward. "Look," I said, "I've got—"

She caught sight of it. Her eyes got real wide. "Did you write me a letter?"

"Not me."

"Did someone write it for you?"

"What? No."

"But it's for me, right?"

"Yes."

"Then can I have it?"

For no good reason, I felt ashamed and looked down. I couldn't even look her in the eye as I handed the letter to her. She took it from my hand and waved it back and forth. It was as if she was teasing me with it—as if to say she had it now and I couldn't take it back.

"It's not from me," I blurted out.

"No?"

"I didn't . . . it's not my letter."

"Who is it from?"

"I'm not supposed to tell you."

"It's a mystery!"

"You could think of it like that."

"But it's not from you?"

"I just said so," I said.

"So you didn't write it?"

"I *said* it's not from me."

"Yes, you did," she said.

"I've got to go—"

"Goodbye, Julian."

"Yeah, goodbye."

"Say my name!"

"Jillian," I said.

"Doesn't that sound weird?"

"What?"

"Julian and Jillian."

"So what?"

"It's like your name is my name inside out."

"I guess."

There was another awkward pause—a long one.

Then she asked, "So that's all you have to say?"

"I gave you the letter. What else do you want?"

"Then I should go to lunch."

"Me too," I said.

"Do you know what's for lunch today?"

"It's Tuesday. That means turkey hash."

"I *hate* turkey hash," she said. "It's so gross."

"Why?"

"Because it's disgusting. It grosses me out."

"I think it's all right," I said.

"Do you want to walk with me to the cafeteria?"

"No, I've got a few things I need to do first. I'll be down in a couple of minutes."

"Then I guess I'll see you in social studies."

"Right."

She started to walk away but then turned around. "That joke about the Indians cracked me up. It even cracked up Mr. Loeb. I was watching him after you said it. He had no right to make you sit in the hall. Your parents pay taxes. You have a right to sit in the classroom."

"I shouldn't have razzed Mr. Caricone," I said.

"No, but Mr. Loeb was still wrong to do that."

"I felt bad afterward."

"Why did you get suspended for a week?"

"What?"

"Did you *really* beat up a kid?"

"What? No! It was just a neighborhood thing. I never laid a hand on anyone."

She smiled at that, like it made a difference. "Goodbye, Julian."

"Goodbye."

"Say my name!"

"Goodbye, Jillian."

"Goodbye, Julian."

I don't know if I've ever felt more relieved when a conversation ended.

Eduardo

It's been two weeks now since I handed Jillian the letter, and Lonnie is getting pretty antsy. I knew this would happen, or something like it. Jillian hasn't said a word about it. It's like the thing never existed, at least as far as she's concerned. She says hello to me every morning, strolls over to my desk to ask me about homework or else just to chat about nothing. But the letter never comes up. It's kind of mean, if you think about it. She knows she's got a secret admirer, but it's like it slipped her mind. No skin off my nose, but Lonnie keeps pumping me for information, and I don't have a clue what's going on with her. He keeps telling me she looks at him weird when he passes her in the hall, like she's figured out what we did. But I'm pretty sure that's just in his head. I've checked out her expression a hundred times in class when she's not looking. There's no difference from before.

Besides, I've got bigger fish to fry. Shlomo Shlomo told me he was playing tag after school a couple of days ago with a new kid named Eduardo. He's from Panama or Honduras or somewhere like that. But the thing is, Shlomo said he's fast. He said I should race him. He said he'd pay to see that race. Except here's the kicker. Shlomo said Eduardo's a *fifth* grader. Which at first I took as a kind of insult. Most of the time, I won't bother to race a fifth grader. But Shlomo's not the type to run his mouth just to hear himself talk. There's usually something to what he says. He said that this kid was not only fast but big, *real* big, and that maybe he got left back a couple of times.

So I decided to have a look at this Eduardo. I didn't want to make a big deal out of it—which meant I couldn't show up with Shlomo because he'd start talking about the race right off, and I wanted to see what I was up against. I waited until after school on Thursday when I knew Shlomo had to rush home for his clarinet lesson. Then I headed out to the playground at the north end of Memorial Field, which is where Shlomo hangs out when he's not hanging out on the block with us.

I don't hang out at Memorial Field a lot because it's lousy with junior high schoolers, and those guys live for the chance to make the rest of us miserable. I've seen it happen time and time again. June rolls around, and a guy graduates from sixth grade, and he's a decent guy, but the next September, as soon as he walks through the front doors at McMasters, he turns into a beast. The only thing I can figure is that there must be something in the water fountains.

So I headed out to Memorial Field for a look at Eduardo. He wasn't hard to find. He was sitting on one end of a seesaw with two fifth graders sitting across from him . . . and it was balanced. He had to be at least six feet tall. I mean, if I didn't get a good look at him, I would've pegged him for a grown-up. But I *did* get a good look. I strolled past the seesaw, minding my own business, and sized him up when he wasn't paying attention. He had no interest in me anyway because he was too busy with his friends, coaching them in Spanish to keep the thing from drifting up or down—or at least, that was what it seemed like from his hand gestures. But then one of his friends started to laugh, and the seesaw started to go down on Eduardo's side, and he peeled off his overcoat, dropped it to the ground, and then he leaned forward, and the seesaw came even again. He was just dead set on keeping that seesaw even. That was a sure sign, in whatever language, that he was a fifth grader. No one but a fifth grader could get so worked up about something so pointless. On the other hand, your average fifth grader doesn't have a mustache, which Eduardo kind of did. It was real faint, like a training-wheel mustache. But it was noticeable. He also had long hair, as long as the Beatles'. It was down to his shoulders.

But here's the thing: *he looked likable.* I know that doesn't paint a word picture of what he looked like. If I were doing a word picture, I'd say he had a dark complexion, with brown eyes and a narrow nose and a large mouth with thick lips—especially the lower lip, which hung down like a flap. It wasn't the features of his face that made him look likable. It was the expression on his face, a kind of wide-open expression. He looked like whatever was going on inside his head would be right there in his eyes. You'd see it floating on the surface, with nothing hidden. I mean, if you think about it, he could've jumped off that seesaw and sent his two friends crashing down—which would be a standard fifth-grader move. But you just knew it was the furthest thing from Eduardo's mind. It wouldn't have occurred to him even if the three of them had been up on that seesaw, in perfect balance, for a million years.

I walked right past the seesaw and sat down at the end of a row of green benches. It was near enough that I could keep an eye on him but still far enough away that he wouldn't notice me. That's what I thought. But then, a couple of minutes later, one of Eduardo's friends got tired of their balancing act and called to him, "C'mon, Eddie. I'm cold. Let's *do* something."

Eduardo heard that, and right then he turned around and looked straight at me. He knew exactly where I was sitting. It turned out he *had* noticed me. He'd noticed me from the start. He smiled and said, "Hello, my friend!"

My first reaction was disbelief. I pointed at myself and said, "Who, me?"

"*Mi amigo.*"

"What do you want?"

"You want to play tag with us, yes?"

"Tag?"

"*Sí*, it will keep us warm."

"What kind of tag?"

The question seemed to throw him. He glanced back at his two friends and spoke with them in Spanish. They spoke back to him in Spanish too. Then he turned again to me. "Just tag."

"Well, I like wolf tag," I said.

"*Wolf* tag?"

"You know. Round-up tag."

"Ah. But we are only four."

"Then you guys go ahead."

He shrugged, then turned again to his friends. "Sorry, Paulo. We don't have enough."

Now Paulo, who had curly hair and thick black glasses, glanced over at me. "C'mon, play with us!"

I sighed to myself. There was no way out. I stood up and pulled off my overcoat.

Eduardo stretched his legs to the ground and let the two of them climb down from the seesaw first, then stepped off himself. The three of them walked over to me. Eduardo had a wide grin on his face. He stuck out his right hand, and I shook it. "My name is Eduardo—"

Paulo cut him off. "But you can call him Eddie."

"These are my good friends Paulo and Hector."

I shook their hands too. It felt like a strange thing to be doing on the playground, shaking hands left and right like we were actors in a play. Hector was around my size, but skinnier. He was as dark-skinned as a Negro kid, which is what I would've taken him for, except his hair was straight. Paulo, the one with glasses and curly hair, was maybe three inches shorter. Eduardo towered over all three of us. I had to keep reminding myself that I was a grade ahead of them.

"I'm Julian."

"Ah, *Julian.*" Eduardo said it as though the *j* were an *h,* and he stretched out the last two syllables to make it sound even more Spanish: *Hooleeahhnnn.* "Do you speak Spanish, *Julian?*"

I shook my head. "Sorry."

"I will teach you, *mi amigo*. That means 'my friend.'"

"*Mi amigo*," I repeated.

He smiled and nodded. "Yes, *mi amigo*. My friend."

Paulo said, "Are we going to play or what?"

"Yes," Eduardo said. He glanced left and right with a sly look on his face. His eyes met mine, but only for a split second. Then, without warning, he poked Paulo on the right shoulder and said, "You're *it*, my friend."

As soon as the words left his mouth, he took off. He looked like he was running in slow motion, like a giraffe. He had real long strides, but he didn't look like he was going real fast. He was graceful, though. There was no denying that. But graceful and fast were two different things. Of course, I was so busy watching him, it didn't occur to me that the game had started. So a second later, I felt Paulo tag me in the chest. "You're it, Julian!"

With that, he and Hector took off. I was left standing by myself. I thought about chasing down one of them, but that didn't seem fair. They were fifth graders. So I trotted in the direction of Eduardo. I figured I'd just feel him out. There was no sense in putting my cards on the table at this point. I trotted after him, and he stood there and waited, and then I got close, and he started to run away from me, and then I took three quick steps . . . and I tagged him.

That was it.

Three quick steps, and I caught him and tagged him.

He turned to me and smiled. "You're a fast runner, *Julian.*"

I stood with my hands on my hips, wondering what had just happened. "I guess."

"Now, where's Hector?"

I glanced over my shoulder. "I think he's back over there, by the monkey bars."

"Yes, I see him. *Gracias.*"

Eduardo ran off in the direction of the monkey bars, and I shook my head. Could Shlomo have been talking about a different Eduardo? What were the chances of two monster-sized fifth graders named Eduardo hanging around Memorial Field? Not likely. But how could Shlomo have gotten the guy so wrong?

The game continued for a few more minutes: Eduardo tagged Hector, and then Hector tagged me. (I let him, just to be a good sport.) Then I tagged Paulo, and then Paulo was about to tag Hector when three junior high school kids showed up out of nowhere and started making trouble. One of them grabbed Paulo by the right arm, and another caught Hector in a bear hug and wouldn't let him go. I was at the far end of the playground when it happened. I wanted to pretend it was none of my business.

Except I recognized one of the junior high schoolers from the block. It was Hiram, Shlomo Shlomo's older brother. He was the one who'd grabbed Paulo by the arm. Now he was twisting the arm behind Paulo's back. The poor kid looked like he was going to bawl.

So I jogged over and said, "C'mon, Hiram. He's a fifth grader."

Hiram looked up at me. "Why don't you run away, Twerski?"

"You think you can catch me?"

"I don't waste my time on the likes of you," he said.

"My friends, my friends . . ." Eduardo had walked up behind me. The sight of him got Hiram's attention, but he wasn't going to back down just yet. "Do you want to play tag with us?"

Hiram glanced at his two buddies. Neither of them looked too pleased at the sight of Eduardo, who was, like, twice the size of the three of them put together. No one knew what to do next. But then one of Hiram's buddies said in a sarcastic way, "You must be their father, right?"

Eduardo just laughed and shook his head. "No, they're my friends."

"So I guess you're in fifth grade."

"Yes."

"What? Are you stupid or something?"

That made Eduardo laugh even harder. *"No, señor."*

Then Hiram said, "You think you can take all three of us?"

"C'mon, he doesn't want to fight," I said.

"I don't remember asking your opinion, *Twerp-ski*."

Eduardo said, "If you want to fight, then yes, I will fight. But I prefer to play tag."

Hiram let go of Paulo's arm. "You *prefer* to play tag?"

"*Sí.*"

Hiram glanced back at his two friends, then took a step toward Eduardo. "What if we prefer to fight?"

Eduardo shrugged. "Very well."

With that, Hiram lowered his head and rushed him. But Eduardo took a quick step backward, then jumped to the side, and Hiram careened past him, lost his balance, and tumbled to the ground.

"*¡Olé!*" Eduardo shouted.

Hiram's two buddies ran at Eduardo, but he sidestepped both of them too. He was a blur. He was there, and then he was gone. Hiram scrambled to his feet, and now the three of them were lunging and grabbing at Eduardo. But they couldn't touch him. I mean it. They couldn't lay a finger on him. It was like a cartoon, like Casper the Ghost. Eduardo seemed like he was made of air.

The weirdest thing was, the entire time, Eduardo never once clenched his fists. He never once stopped smiling. It was as if he *was* still playing tag. He wasn't going to fight them. He just wanted to dodge them until they gave up. Whenever one of them got close, he cried, *"¡Olé!"* That made them even madder.

Soon, Hiram and his friends were huffing and gagging. They were staggering after Eduardo, not even rushing him anymore. Hiram's face looked like a pitcher of cherry Kool-Aid, that's how red it was. I thought he was going to have a heart attack. The end came when he stopped and bent over, gasping for air. His friends stopped too. The three of them stood with their hands on their knees, spitting onto the ground. Between coughs, Hiram managed to say, "You're a foreign freak. That's what you are."

Eduardo gave a slight laugh, then stepped past them. He hadn't even broken a sweat. He snatched up his overcoat, which was still lying in a heap next to the seesaw, and led Paulo and Hector out of the playground. As the three of them were walking away, he turned and winked at me.

The truth hit me like a sledgehammer. I felt it right in my guts: *Eduardo had let me tag him.*

Shlomo hadn't been wrong about Eduardo. He was the fastest kid I'd ever seen.

March 5, 1969

Mrs. Fine

Let me tell you, Selkirk is lapping this stuff up. (Sorry, Mr. Selkirk, but it's the truth, and we both know it.) After the story about Quentin's eyebrows, he said I sounded like a Jewish Tom Sawyer. I just nodded at that, as if it made perfect sense to me. Or as if I were writing about being Jewish—which I haven't even mentioned, not even once, so I don't know where he gets that. Really and truly, Mr. Selkirk, I don't know where you get that.

Sure, I've got the Big B next year. Bar mitzvah, I mean. I don't put a lot of stock in it, though. I'll get up in temple, and I'll say the words I'm supposed to say. I owe my mom and dad that much. But to me Hebrew school is just more school. Except it's like being stuck in first grade, over and over. You're back to figuring out letters and sounding out words, learning how to print and then how to write cursive. What's the point? English is what I speak. It's what my friends speak. It's what I'm going to keep speaking, unless I move to Israel, which is about as likely as Bernard Segal starting in center field for the Mets.

The worst part of Hebrew school is that Rabbi Salzberg makes such a big deal out of it. He's always saying how regular school is for your brain but Hebrew school is for your brain *and* your heart. I mean, he could just say that and be done with it. But he makes it into a regular performance. He makes the entire class stand up, and he asks, "Where does *school* make you smart?" Then we've all got to point at our heads. After that, he asks, "But where does *shul* make you smart?" Then we've all got to point at our heads and then at our hearts. Then he smiles and says, "Exactly right!" Unless, of course, one of us isn't pointing hard enough. Then Salzberg rushes over to him and starts poking him in the chest over and over, saying, "Can you feel it? Can you feel the Torah *in here*?"

"Yes, Rabbi, I can feel it. . . ."

The Jewish thing is a much bigger deal for Lonnie on account of his mom. She was in a concentration camp. The Germans cut her tongue in half. She had four surgeries, and now she can talk all right—except it sounds painful. Kind of forced and wet. Plus, she's got an accent, so it's hard to understand her. Not that she talks a lot. She's real nice to us, though. She'll fix Lonnie whatever he wants, even if it's a half hour before dinner. She'll whip out a box of Mallomars like it's nothing. My mom says we should be ashamed of ourselves, taking advantage of Mrs. Fine. But I don't look at it as taking advantage. That's just how she is. Good-natured.

My mom plays mah-jongg with Mrs. Fine. There's about seven or eight ladies who rotate in and out of their games. It's a loud game, mah-jongg. Especially if you're trying to fall asleep in the next room. There's the clatter of tiles, plus the sound of ladies yelling "One crak!" and "Two bam!" Mrs. Fine sometimes has trouble getting the words out, and it slows down the game. But the rest of the ladies don't seem to mind.

I know it bugs my mom, though. There was this one night when Mrs. Fine kept getting stuck and saying how sorry she was. Later that night, after the game was over and the ladies had gone home, I heard my mom crying in bed, and my dad telling her not to dwell on it. There was nothing she could do for her.

Mrs. Fine goes to temple every Saturday morning. She's there whenever I'm there—which is about once every month or so when Rabbi Salzberg gets after me about it. But even when I'm not there, I know Mrs. Fine is because she walks past our house going there and back. I've never known her to miss, not even once. She used to drag Lonnie with her, and he used to drag me, but now he's old enough to be left alone, so she goes by herself—Mr. Fine doesn't go with her because he's too busy at the candy store.

But you should see Mrs. Fine in temple. It's a big deal for her. She doesn't just bow her head and peek at her watch like the rest of us. She gets worked up. She knows the entire service backward and forward. She sits in the front row with her eyes shut tight, mouthing the Hebrew words even before the rabbi says them out loud. She rocks back and forth, like she's in a trance. She clenches and unclenches her fists. Then, toward the end, when the rabbi gets to *Shema Yisrael,* she jerks her head back, and she's got this real alive expression. It's like she's in a fight, and she's getting whaled on. I don't know why she goes, to be honest. I don't know what she gets out of it. As far as I can tell, it just makes her sad.

Lonnie's dad, like I said, doesn't go to temple too often because he's working at the candy store. He's plenty religious, though. When Lonnie got a dog three years ago, Mr. Fine named him Lord. Can you believe that? *Lord!* What kind of name is that for a dog? It's almost an insult if you stop and think about it. To God, I mean. I'm sure the dog doesn't care one way or another. He's a Shetland sheepdog, which is a slightly smaller version of a collie.

He's a good dog, not too barky or drooly. But the name ruins it. I mean, how can you say, "Sit, Lord! Sit! Roll over, Lord!" without it sounding funny coming out of your mouth?

The last time I went to temple for a good reason was Lonnie's bar mitzvah. He said his haftarah all right. No major errors that I could tell. After he finished, Rabbi Salzberg walked across the stage, put his arm around Lonnie's shoulders, and told him what it means to be a Jew: going to services each Saturday, keeping kosher, marrying a nice Jewish girl, bringing up nice Jewish children. The entire time, Lonnie had a *yeah, right* look on his face. I could tell he just wanted to get down off that stage and get on with his life.

But ever since then, he keeps getting dragged into minyans. That's when old Jewish guys get together to say prayers—not even in temple. They get together in one of their basements—and then they sit around for an hour and talk about stuff like what it means to be a Jew. (Jews talk about that *a lot*.) I've never been to one because you're not allowed until after your bar mitzvah. That's another reason I'm not looking forward to mine.

The catch is that you need at least ten Jews for a minyan, and the Jewish dads don't get home early enough from work, and the Jewish moms aren't allowed because they're women, so it's just the geezers and whatever poor suckers they can rope into doing it. It's the one time I feel sorry for the junior high schoolers. The weird thing is, Lonnie would be in junior high himself except he had to repeat sixth grade. I half think he flunked so he could wait around for Quentin, Eric, Howie, Shlomo, and me. But to get back to what I was saying, you should see the junior high schoolers duck for cover whenever the geezer patrol starts to scour the neighborhood, looking for that tenth Jew.

Lonnie keeps getting caught because he refuses to hide out. He just keeps on doing what he's doing, and if the geezers find him, he takes his medicine. But he goofs on them afterward like no one's business. He hunches over like he's a hundred years old and clears his throat so loud you'd think he was about to cough up a lung, and then he starts saying, "Oy, de pain! Oy, de pain!" It's downright hysterical. He cracks me up every time.

Amelia's Room

I know you don't care about Mrs. Fine, Mr. Selkirk. I know you're still waiting for me to write about what happened with Danley Dimmel . . . and I know I'm not supposed to call him that, even though that's what the entire neighborhood calls him. Maybe that's not right. Maybe, if the world were perfect, no one would call him that. Then again, if the world were perfect, he wouldn't have been born hard of hearing and soft in the head. He would've been able to say his own name, and "Stanley Stimmel" wouldn't have come out "Danley Dimmel."

But the world *isn't* perfect, and that's what happened, so that's what kids call him. That's what he calls himself. Even though he can talk all right now, on account of his hearing aid, he still calls himself that. It's his nickname.

What I mean is, he *likes* it. You know how I know? Because I've heard him say "Stanley Stimmel." I was walking past his house a couple of years ago, and he was sitting out on his stoop, which is all he ever does, and there was a substitute mailman, and he asked Danley what his name was, and Danley said "Stanley Stimmel." It was clear as a bell, the way he said it: "Stanley Stimmel." But he calls himself Danley Dimmel if he's talking to a kid. I figure it's a guy's choice to be called what he wants to be called. So if he wants to be called Danley Dimmel, that's what I'm going to call him.

But it doesn't matter what I call him, or what I don't call him, if you want to know the truth, because I don't talk to him. No one talks to him, which is the reason he sits by himself on the stoop. That sounds mean, I know. You could be dramatic about it and say no one likes him. But no one *dislikes* him either. He's just not the kind of guy you have an opinion about . . . and, no, it's not because he goes to a different school. Quentin went to that school for a year before his mom raised hell and got him out, and you'll never hear anyone say anything bad about Quentin.

It might be different if Danley were a couple of years younger. If he were closer to our age, and if he weren't the size of an elephant, he might be hanging around with us in Ponzini. Who knows? He might be like Quentin, and no one would say a bad word about him. But that's not the way things worked out.

The way things worked out, no one cares about Danley. *I* don't care about Danley. There, I've said it. You can flunk me in English, or do whatever to me, but nothing is going to change that. I wish what happened to Danley didn't happen. But it did happen, and it's not like I'm losing sleep over it. You want to know what I'm losing sleep over?

Eduardo.

Maybe that makes me a shallow person, the fact that I couldn't fall asleep until after midnight for three nights in a row because I was lying in bed, worrying about whether I was still the fastest kid in P.S. 23. If that makes me a shallow person, then all right. I'm a shallow person.

When I got home from Memorial Field that afternoon I met Eduardo, I felt sick to my stomach. My mom's stuffed cabbage had no taste, at least not to me. As I shoveled the last forkful down my throat, she asked me if I'd had a rough day at school. What was I supposed to tell her? *Yeah, Mom, you could say I had a rough day. But it's all right because at least I'm still the second-fastest kid at school . . . unless Eduardo has a twin brother, in which case I'm the third-fastest.*

Do you want to know what I've figured out in the two weeks since then? The only thing people care about is whatever they happen to care about. What I mean is, they care about their own stuff. Take you, Mr. Selkirk. You care about Danley Dimmel and what happened to him, and what I'm writing or not writing about it. You said so yourself in our talk on Monday. That's *your* stuff.

Lonnie, on the other hand, cares about Jillian. That's *his* stuff. It's all he wants to talk about, all he wants to hear about. I wish I'd never written that letter for him, if you want to know the honest truth. I feel for him, for sure, but I knew nothing good was going to come of that letter, and I told him so, and he did what he felt like doing—or rather, *he got me to do* what he felt like doing—and now it's turned out just like I thought it would. Worse, in a way. Because Jillian *still* hasn't asked me who wrote the letter, hasn't shown the slightest interest in knowing since I handed it to her last month. On the other hand, she'll come up to me during a break and ask if I wrote down the homework assignment in math or if she can copy the notes I took in social studies. Even though she sat through both classes the same as I did. But as for the letter, not a word. It's like the entire incident got erased from her memory. Which would be fine with me, except it didn't get erased from Lonnie's memory. Truthfully, I wish she'd just torn up the letter and flung it back in my face. That way, at least I'd know what to tell him.

The latest brainstorm he had was for me to ask Amelia

what to do next. That's about the last thing I want to do, bring Amelia in on it. But Lonnie said that women understand one another, that there's a secret language going on between them that guys don't pick up on. He has no idea how squirmy that kind of conversation is because he doesn't have an older sister. Or brother. Lonnie's an only child, so he just figures it's a five-minute talk, in and out, no consequences. But trust me. There are *always* consequences. Not for him. He just gets free advice. But Amelia will lord it over me for the next year, at least. That's how it works.

I don't even like to go into Amelia's room. You know how normal seventeen-year-old girls like to hang posters of Davy Jones and Desi Arnaz Jr. and Bobby Sherman? Well, Amelia likes to tape up the posters and then scribble on them with a red magic marker. Like, she'll scribble across Davy Jones's face, "What a corporate lie!" and across Bobby Sherman's face, "Ever heard of Vietnam?" Where she doesn't have posters taped up, the walls are full of beads. That girl loves beads! Pink. Purple. Light blue. She's hammered about a dozen nails into her walls at different heights and with different-colored beads hanging down from them. If she opens a window to let a breeze in, the entire room rattles. My dad cuts her a lot of slack, but even he jokes about it sometimes. He calls her the fortune-teller on account of what her room looks like.

So I had a bad feeling as I knocked at her door. She had a Jefferson Airplane record on her stereo, and I heard her scramble off the bed and turn down the volume right after I knocked. She must have thought it was our mom, who's always telling her to turn down the stereo. The expression on her face when she opened the door seemed to say, *Oh, it's just you.* But then, a second later, the expression changed. Maybe she could tell that I wasn't there because I wanted to be there. Whatever the reason, her expression went soft. She swung her head to the left, which meant I had permission to enter her room.

I sat down on the bed, and she sat down on the rolling chair at her desk. She smiled at me in an agreeable way. But at first I didn't talk. I couldn't figure out how to start the conversation. Maybe five seconds passed, and she began to roll her eyes. "Are you a leprechaun?"

"What?"

"Are you here to do a jig for Saint Patrick's Day?"

I blurted out, "I need advice."

"What about?"

"It's about school."

"You didn't get suspended again, did you?"

"What? No, it's nothing like that."

"Good," she said. "Because that's not you."

"How do you know?"

"I know *you*, Julian. You're not the kind of kid—"

I cut her off. "I just need advice. Are you going to help me out or not?"

"You're not having problems with your homework, are you?"

"No, it's not about homework."

"Then what's it about?"

I turned my head to the side. Even as the words were coming out, I didn't want to say them. "It's about . . . a girl."

She got a huge grin on her face. "You're putting me on."

"C'mon, Amelia, I need advice!"

"This is *so* adorable," she said.

"It's not adorable. It's serious."

She rolled her chair closer. "Talk to me, little brother."

I couldn't even look her in the eye. "Would you back up a couple of feet?"

She laughed and rolled the chair in reverse. "How's this?"

I looked up and nodded. "Better."

"So what's her name?"

"Jillian."

"You've got the hots for her?"

"What? No!"

"I'm sorry. I didn't mean to say 'the hots.' That's the wrong word for sixth grade."

"It's not me. It's . . . a friend."

"So your *friend* is really into this girl Jillian?"

"Don't say it like that."

"Say what like what?"

"Don't say 'friend' like you think I'm talking about myself."

She smiled. She didn't believe me for a second. "So your friend, who's not you, is really into this Jillian chick?"

"Yes."

"Does Jillian like him?"

"I don't know. I don't think so."

"Why not?"

"Because he wrote her a letter."

"And?"

"She never even answered him."

"That's not a good sign," she said. "What did you write in the letter?"

"Just some stuff about how nice she is."

"So you admit it's you!"

"What? No!"

"C'mon, you just admitted it—"

"No, I didn't."

"I asked what *you* wrote in the letter, and you said you wrote about how nice she is."

"Maybe I wrote it for someone else," I said. "Did that ever cross your mind?"

"Did you write it for Quentin?"

"What difference does it make who I wrote it for?"

"I'm guessing you didn't write it for Lonnie. He would've written his own letter."

"Does it matter?"

"Yes, it matters," she said. "Quentin is cute. Lonnie isn't."

"Guys aren't *cute*."

"Not to other guys. But to girls they are. Some of them."

"Why is Quentin cute, but not Lonnie?"

"Quentin has doe eyes. Lonnie is more of a schemer."

I thought about what she was saying, about whether it could be true. "But you're seventeen. Girls my age might have a different opinion."

"Trust me on this one, Julian. I remember what it's like to be twelve. You have *no idea* how well I remember what it's like."

"All right."

"So did you write the letter for Quentin or not?"

"Let's say I did."

"Did you try to sound like Quentin, or did you just write it in your own voice?"

"I wrote a letter saying how nice she was. I wasn't trying to sound like anyone."

"Can I read the letter?"

"No!"

"All right! No need to get hostile!"

"Amelia—"

"I'm only trying to figure out if you fooled her. Quentin wouldn't use the same words you would use. He doesn't have your vocabulary. What I mean is . . . Look, I love Quentin. He's my favorite of your friends. But let's face facts. He's not Einstein. Every girl who knows him knows that. The fact that he's sweet makes up for it, but it's still the truth. So if Jillian has figured out that Quentin didn't write his own letter, she's not going to answer him. Why should she? Quentin hasn't put himself out there. He hasn't made himself vulnerable."

"Then you don't think she's ever going to write back to him?"

"Why would she write back if she knows it wasn't his letter?"

"Because it's wrong to leave a guy hanging like that," I said.

"Then tell me this: Are you sure she *got* the letter?"

"Yes."

"How do you know?"

"Because I'm the one who handed it to her."

"*You* handed it to her?"

"Yes."

"Did you tell her who it was from?"

"I told her I didn't write it."

"Except you *did* write it," she said.

"Yes, but I told her I didn't."

"Did you specifically tell her it was from a secret admirer?"

"I didn't use the exact words. But she knew what I meant."

"Interesting." Amelia tapped her left index finger against her chin. "Has she talked to you since then?"

"She talks to me all the time," I said. "I think she talks to me more now than she ever did before. That's what makes the situation so annoying. If she just gave me a hint what she thought about the letter—"

Suddenly, Amelia brought her hands to her face. "Oh my God! You're an idiot!"

"Why am I an idiot?"

"The reason Jillian hasn't answered the letter is she thinks it's from you."

"But I *told* her it wasn't from me."

"She's given you her answer in person," Amelia said. "The answer is that she's interested . . . in *you*. You stole Quentin's girl."

"I did not!"

"I'm not saying you did it on purpose. I'm saying that's what happened."

"I knew this was a mistake!"

"It's three mistakes," she said. "Quentin never should have asked you to write a letter for him. You never should have done it. But you *never* should have handed Jillian the letter yourself. That's the dumbest mistake. Of course she thinks you wrote it. What else is she going to think?"

"I meant it was a mistake to ask your advice."

She raised her palms in the air. "Hey, don't shoot the messenger."

"There's *no way* Jillian thinks I wrote that letter."

"There's no way she doesn't, Julian." She narrowed her eyes at me, then began to laugh. "Hmm, Julian and Jillian. Sounds to me like the two of you were meant to be together."

She was still cracking up as I walked out of her room.

Waiting for the Bus

As stupid as what Amelia said was, it's the kind of thing that gets under your skin. I couldn't let go of it. The conversation I had with Jillian when I first handed her the letter—I must have replayed it a million times in my mind. (It helped that I wrote most of it down. I guess that's another advantage of doing this kind of assignment. Not only does it get you out of writing a report on *Julius Caesar*, it's also a great reminder.) So I read back what I wrote, and there it was in black and white: I told Jillian flat out I didn't write the letter. She would have to be as stupid as Amelia to think I did.

So I had what Amelia said under my skin, and I had that wink from Eduardo under my skin, and there's just so many things that can fit under your skin at a given moment without driving you crazy. I had to get rid of something. I decided just to ask Jillian about the letter. But deciding to do it and doing it are two different things. I must have taken a first step in her direction a half-dozen times and chickened out. That was another two weeks of grief. But then, at last, I caught up with her while she was waiting for the yellow bus to Bayside. The fact that she was standing off by herself, not quite in line with the rest of the kids, seemed like a good sign. I gritted my teeth and came up behind her.

I tapped her on the shoulder, and she turned around. Then she gave me that same wide-eyed look as when I first handed her the letter.

"Can I talk to you for a minute?" I said.

Her eyes got even bigger. "Yes."

"Do you remember that letter I gave you?"

"Yes."

"What did you think about it?"

"I thought it was beautiful," she said.

"That's it?"

"I thought it was very beautiful."

"But what did you think?"

"I just told you."

"What I mean is, do you think . . ."

I couldn't figure out how to finish the sentence.

"Say what you want to say, Julian."

"I don't know what I want to say."

"You don't have to be shy. I won't bite."

"Look, my friend just wants to know—"

She spun around and turned her back to me.

Before I could think what to do next, I heard a voice behind me. "*Hola,* Jillian!"

She turned back around and smiled. "Eduardo!"

He trotted up to the bus stop. Even at a slow trot, he seemed to glide. "*¡Julian! ¿Cómo estás?*"

As shocked as I was to see him, what happened next shocked me even more. He slid his arm around Jillian's waist and gave her a kiss on the right cheek. Then he gave her a kiss on the left cheek. Then she turned to me, smiling again. His arm was still around her waist. "Do you know Eduardo, Julian?"

"What? No . . . um, yes."

"Eduardo, this is Julian."

"*Mi amigo,*" he said.

"Eduardo is my brother."

"What?"

"He's not my real brother," Jillian said.

Eduardo cracked up but didn't speak.

"He lives with us. He's from Guatemala."

He let go of her waist and put out his hand. I shook it again.

"My parents want to adopt him," she said, "so he might be my real brother by next year."

"No one knows what the future will be, Jillian."

"Eduardo is a great soccer player. He could be a professional."

He wagged his finger at her. "What is this word, 'soccer'?"

"All right, I mean *fútbol*."

"*Muy bien*, Jillian."

"*Gracias.*"

"*De nada.*"

"Eduardo is teaching me Spanish . . . *español.*"

"So Eduardo lives with you?" I said, even though she'd just told me that he did. I wanted to hear her say it again.

"Yes, my dad made a room for him in the cellar. He sleeps on a sofa bed. He doesn't even have to make it in the morning. He just folds it up and puts the cushions back in place. Plus, he has his own bathroom."

"It's excellent, *Julian*. You must come over and see it."

Jillian's eyes just bugged out when he said that. "Yes!"

"Yes, what?" I said.

"You must come over and see Eduardo's room."

"Yes, you must, *Julian*!"

My mind was a blur at that moment. Up until then,

I had Eduardo worries, and I had Jillian worries, and the two were separate. Like two rivers running through the back of my mind. But now, at once, they came together. It was like a rushing, tumbling waterfall of confusion, and I was trying to keep an expression on my face that looked as if nothing was going on.

I heard Jillian say, "What about this Saturday?"

"¡Sábado!"

The two of them were right in front of my face, smiling, hopeful that I would say yes, and I was figuring out an excuse—grasping for one, to be honest, no matter how fake, no matter how lame. But then I had a moment of inspiration. The scene at the bus stop seemed to slow down, and the roaring waterfall inside my head became a normal stream. It was me again, my voice, not a waterfall. I knew what I was going to say. "Can I bring a friend?"

The question seemed to catch them both off guard. They glanced at one another out of the corners of their eyes. They were still smiling at me, but I could tell that neither of them knew what to say next, whether to answer the question alone or come up with one answer together. It felt good to mess them up. Then at last Jillian said, "That depends who your friend is."

"Just a guy from the block."

"A boy?"

"Why would I bring a girl?"

That made Jillian smile again. "Sure, you can bring your friend."

"¡Bien!" Eduardo said.

Jillian whipped out a piece of loose-leaf paper and wrote down her address, then handed it to Eduardo, who handed it to me. It was like she was saying the invitation was from both of them.

"That's the address," she said. "It's on Twenty-Ninth Avenue, a block from Francis Lewis Boulevard. Do you know where that is?"

"I know it's way out in Bayside."

"Do you know how to get there?"

"I'll figure it out," I said.

The yellow bus turned the corner and rolled up the street toward the stop. Jillian nodded at it. "You should come over for lunch. One o'clock? If it's warm enough outside, my dad might even barbecue. That's what he loves doing. Is that all right? Do you like barbecue?"

"Yeah, I do."

Which was the truth.

The bus pulled up at the stop, and the driver cranked the doors open. Eduardo thrust out his hand. That seemed to be his thing, shaking hands—first at Memorial Field, when it made sense, and now here, for no reason. But what the heck? I shook his hand again. For no reason. Then Jillian put out her hand, and I shook hers too. It felt real soft, real weak, with nothing behind it, almost like it wasn't there. I wasn't certain if she was making fun of me, or of Eduardo, or of both of us, but I shook her hand regardless. Why not?

I watched them climb onto the school bus. They took the first seat behind the bus driver, which no one in his right mind ever does, and they were chattering away when the yellow doors slammed shut. As the bus drove off, I turned and headed home.

April 6, 1969

Sábado

You should've seen the look on Lonnie's face when I told him the two of us were invited to Jillian's house for lunch. He thought it was an April Fools' joke at first—which I would never do, given how he feels about her. But I convinced him it was real. Except then I figured he needed to know about Eduardo. That brought him back to earth fast. We were in front of the Hampshire House, waiting for Quentin to come downstairs. As soon as I told him about Eduardo, Lonnie started pacing back and forth. He didn't like the sound of Jillian's Guatemalan "brother," not one bit, and to be honest, I couldn't blame him.

It just didn't seem right, the two of them under the same roof. There are things that happen when you live with someone, accidental things. For example, and it grosses me out to mention it, but I can't count the number of times I've seen Amelia in her underwear. It just happens. Like we'll both shuffle out to the refrigerator from opposite ends of the apartment in the middle of the night, and one of us will turn on the kitchen light, and then there we are . . . and I'm in my pajamas, and she's in her underwear. Then, of course, she runs back into her room and yells at me to get lost, which wakes up my mom and dad. But it's not her fault or my fault. It just happens because we live under the same roof.

Now think how weird it must be for Jillian and Eduardo, who aren't even related to one another, to meet up in the kitchen in the middle of the night. Plus, you just *know* Eduardo's the kind of guy who sleeps in his underwear, not in pajamas. If I were Lonnie, that thought would bug the heck out of me.

Lonnie started pumping me for more information about Eduardo, and I told him what I knew—everything except him being fast, which I figured was between me and Eduardo. But I told Lonnie how likable he was, how he stood up to the junior high school kids—though I didn't go into details—how he looked you straight in the eye and smiled, and how he called you *"amigo."*

Lonnie thought it over, then said, "In other words, the guy's a phony."

"No, I think he means it. I think he's just likable."

"No one's that likable. Trust me, he only wants you to *think* he's likable."

"Then he's doing a good job," I said, "because I do."

"That doesn't prove a thing. You're *way* too trusting."

There was no point in arguing with him. He hadn't even met the guy.

"So are you going to come or not?"

"Sure, I'll come. But I'm keeping a close eye on this Eduardo creep."

Just as he said that, Quentin showed up. That ended the conversation.

Saturday afternoon rolled around, and Lonnie and I caught the Bayside bus to Francis Lewis Boulevard. It was definitely warm enough for a barbecue. As a matter of fact, it was ridiculously hot, like eighty-five degrees. It felt as if a July day had wandered into the first week of April.

The bus ride was full of rattles and bumps. It set my nerves on edge, but not as much as Lonnie did. He had on a white shirt and dark blue tie. I'd seen him in ties before, at school assemblies and at his bar mitzvah, but I'd never seen him like that. The knot was so tight that it looked like his head was going to explode. Plus, it was making him sweat. You could see beads of sweat on his forehead and the tip of his nose. He also had on blue dress pants with a straight crease and a thick black belt, which was also about two notches too tight. He looked about as stiff and uncomfortable as a guy could get.

It made me feel kind of weird, how dressed up he was, because I had on blue jeans and a T-shirt. But what could I do? I couldn't go home and change at that point.

I tried to talk to him during the bus ride, just casual talk about nothing, but he kept waving me off and staring out the window. It was like he was about to die, like the Grim Reaper was hanging around outside the bus window, showing Lonnie his life frame by frame, showing him where he'd gone wrong. It takes a lot to spook Lonnie, but he was as spooked as I'd ever seen him.

Just to snap him out of it, I elbowed him in the side. He turned to me with a sad look in his eyes. "What?"

"It's not a big deal."

"I know," he said.

"It's just a Saturday afternoon."

He looked at me in a hopeful way. "Am I making too big a deal out of it?"

"By a lot," I said.

"Because it feels like I am."

"You are. Trust me."

"But what if it *is* a big deal?"

"How could it be a big deal?"

"What if Jillian is the girl I wind up marrying?"

"You're thirteen years old! For crying out loud!"

"But—"

"Lonnie, you're *not* marrying Jillian—"

"But how do you know that for sure?"

"You're not marrying her *today*. So relax."

He looked at me in a curious way, as if what I'd said was real deep and he was struggling to get his mind around it. But it was just common sense. If his brain was right, Lonnie would've been the first to realize that. Which goes to show how love messes up your brain. It worms itself in there, inside your brain, and then there's a short circuit. I'm no expert on the subject. I'm just going by Howie and Lonnie. Love makes great guys into idiots.

He went back to staring out the bus window, but after another minute he turned to me and said, "So you don't think that there's something fishy going on with this Eduardo?"

"No, I don't."

I said that, but I had no idea *what* was going on between the two of them. Except I wasn't going to tell Lonnie that and make him even more crazy. The truth is, right then, I was thinking that maybe bringing Lonnie along to Jillian's house wasn't such a good idea. But I figured putting him and her together in one room was a kill or cure deal. Either he would talk to her and figure out she wasn't interested, or he would talk to her and the two of them would hit it off. Whichever way it went, I'd be off the hook. Then I would just have Eduardo to worry about.

Jillian's house is pretty snazzy. It puts the houses on Thirty-Fourth Avenue to shame. Not that Thirty-Fourth Avenue isn't nice. But it's got mostly six-story apartment buildings and two-family houses, with only a few stand-alones mixed in. But none of them were like Jillian's house. It looked like a gingerbread house, with a tall pointed brown roof over the front door and stone walls instead of brick. It just looked real solid, like a tornado could've hit it straight on and not made a dent in the thing.

As soon as we turned up the path to the front door, Eduardo and Jillian stepped outside to meet us.

"*¡Amigos!*" Eduardo called.

"What did I tell you?" I muttered, just loud enough for Lonnie to hear.

Except Lonnie seemed like he didn't hear a word I'd said. I don't think he even noticed Eduardo. He was too focused on Jillian. I couldn't blame him, to be honest. She had on a white T-shirt and white shorts, and her dark brown hair was flowing out behind her, fluttering in the breeze. Plus, she was smiling, so the sunlight was shining on her white teeth. She looked like a model in a magazine.

She took another couple of steps forward, nothing dramatic, but the sight of her froze Lonnie in his tracks. It was like he hit an invisible wall. I could hear the air go out of him. I glanced over at him, and he was behind me. It was just sad. But slightly comical at the same time. I didn't know whether to stop or to keep walking. Eduardo made the decision for me. He jogged down the rest of the path, past Jillian, and put out his hand. For once, I was glad to shake it.

"Who is your friend, *Julian?*" he said in a loud voice.

"That's Lonnie."

He let go of my hand and then walked up to Lonnie with his hand out. The sight of the two of them shaking hands came as a shock. It shouldn't have, I suppose, but it did. The way Eduardo towered over Lonnie—mind you, Lonnie's a pretty tall guy himself—made the fact that Eduardo was only in fifth grade even more unbelievable. It was just unfair. That's the only word for it. Why should I have to run against a guy that size? His legs were like twice as long as mine. If I were that tall, I'd be running against giraffes. That's how fast I would be.

It just wasn't fair.

Shaking hands with Eduardo seemed to snap Lonnie out of the trance he was in, maybe because looking up at Eduardo forced him to take his eyes off of Jillian, or maybe because he hated Eduardo from that first moment. It probably wasn't obvious to Eduardo or Jillian. But if you knew Lonnie, you could see the hatred wash across his face. The way his eyes narrowed, the way his head crooked to the left, the way he was smiling at Eduardo, it was poisonous.

"Hi, Lonnie," Jillian called, but she didn't step forward.

Lonnie gave her a quick wave. That was it. Just a wave.

"My dad's got the grill going in the backyard," she said, then waved us forward. "C'mon!"

Instead of going back into the house, she cut across the front lawn. She walked over to a high wooden fence on the left, between the house and the driveway, slipped a metal latch, and pulled open the gate. Eduardo, Lonnie, and I watched her. Then Eduardo trotted through the gate after her. Lonnie's eyes met mine for a split second, as if he had a question for me, but I had no idea what the question was, let alone the answer. I had no idea what to do except follow Eduardo and Jillian around the house and into the backyard.

The first thing we saw in the backyard was a swimming pool. It wasn't a big one, maybe twenty-five feet by ten feet, but the surface of the water was glistening in the sun. Mr. Rifkin was standing in front of a round grill at the near end of the pool, six feet from the edge of the water. He was tall and thin, with a long forehead shaped like a shoehorn and black frizzy hair. You know how sometimes you can tell about a person the second you lay eyes on him? Jillian's dad was a goofball. I don't know how else to describe him. He had on white socks and green thong sandals. He also had on a long Hawaiian shirt and green Bermuda shorts, plus an apron that said MASTER GRILLER.

I just knew, if I glanced back at Lonnie, the two of us were going to crack up, so I kept my eyes forward.

Down at the far end of the pool, on a lounge chair, was Jillian's mom. She was lying on her stomach, sunbathing. She was as close to naked as I've ever seen a grown-up. Her back was covered with suntan oil. She was just marinating in the stuff, and she had on a pink bikini, and the top of it wasn't even tied. The pink strings dangled off her shoulders. When I saw what she looked like, and then I thought about what the moms on Thirty-Fourth Avenue looked like, there was no comparison. I mean, Mrs. Rifkin looked like a movie star, like Raquel Welch or Elizabeth Taylor. Her skin was just so smooth. I don't know if she realized Jillian's guests had come into the backyard. She sure didn't make a move to say hello. *That*, I would have noticed.

I tried not to stare at Mrs. Rifkin, or at Mr. Rifkin, or at the pool, or at Jillian or Eduardo. There was nothing in that entire backyard that I could focus my eyes on that didn't make me feel uncomfortable.

Then I heard Jillian call to her father, "Dad, company!"

That made him look up from the grill. He noticed

Lonnie and me, and he waved with the metal spatula still in his hand. "Hi there, boys! Welcome to *la casa Rifkin!*" He tried trilling the letter *r* at the start of "*Rifkin,*" but it sounded more like he was clearing his throat. The grin on his face was pure goofball. "Either of you young guns bring a suit?"

For a second, I didn't know what he meant. Then I realized he was talking about a *bathing* suit. I shook my head.

"Too bad," he said. "Sweet day for a swim."

He might have been right, but how were *we* supposed to know Jillian had a pool at her house? She'd never mentioned it, and neither had Eduardo. Besides, I wasn't going near that pool with Mrs. Rifkin lying there greased up and pretty much naked. She still hadn't moved a muscle since we came through the gate. I even thought she might be deaf, given how loud her husband's voice was when he said hello. It seemed strange that she didn't at least wave at us. That was the natural thing to do. It seemed kind of rude, to be honest.

Just then, Eduardo came up behind me and grabbed my hand. I don't think I'd ever had a guy grab my hand before—except maybe my dad, when I was a kid, and he was about to walk me across the street.

"Come, *Julian,*" he said, "I will show you where I live."

I glanced over my shoulder. "What about Lonnie?"

But Lonnie shook his head. "No, you guys go ahead."

"Are you going to be all right?" I asked.

That made Lonnie laugh. "You think an alligator's going to get me?"

"Well, no—"

"You go right ahead, *Julian.*" The way he said my name sounded just like the way Eduardo said it. Even Eduardo cracked up at how Lonnie could imitate his voice so fast.

If I'd let him, I think Eduardo might have led me by the hand the entire way down to the cellar. But after a couple of steps I slowed up, and he let go. It just didn't feel right, holding a guy's hand . . . it felt kind of girlish. But I followed him down the stairs and into the cellar. The way he talked up the place, I expected the Taj Mahal. It turned out to be just the corner of a wood-paneled cellar with a beat-up convertible couch, a wicker trunk, a dented metal folding chair, and a rickety wooden desk that doubled as a nightstand. The light was bad. There was only a sliver of sunlight coming through a ground-level window the size of a shoe box and a bare lightbulb that hung from the ceiling with a chain to turn it on and off. As for stuff, he had a soccer ball and a transistor radio shaped like a miniature soccer ball. As far as I could tell, that was it.

I walked back and forth, taking in the place. Meanwhile, he sat on the edge of the convertible couch and waited for my reaction. I could tell he was real interested. He wanted me to like it.

"It's pretty nice," I said. "But doesn't it get hot down here?"

"*Señor Rifkin* says he will put in a fan during the summer."

"What about until then?"

"In my country, it is very warm," he said. "I'm used to it."

"You're from Guatemala, right?"

He smiled at me. "*Sí, señor.*"

"Why did you leave?"

"I met Jillian's father two years ago. He liked me very much, and he said for me to come to America."

"What do you mean, he 'said' for you to come to America?"

"He did arrangements for me. It was very difficult, I think."

"How did you meet him?"

"He came to the orphanage."

"You lived in an orphanage?"

"*Sí, señor,*" he said.

"What happened to your parents?"

The question caught him off guard. He didn't answer for several seconds, then said, "It is all right that you ask, *Julian.* But that I cannot talk about."

"Why not?"

"It hurts me," he said. "It hurts my heart."

What came next caught *me* off guard. Tears started rolling out of the corners of his eyes. He wasn't bawling, exactly. He wasn't shaking or sobbing the way you do when you're bawling. He had a kind of half smile. But tears were rolling down his cheeks in two thin streams. I thought about the hundreds of times my dad or mom had lectured me on how good I had it, on how much I took for granted . . . and I'd just shrugged them off. But here was living proof. Whatever had happened to Eduardo back in Guatemala, whatever had happened to his parents, it must've been real bad. He must've seen real bad stuff. I felt pretty low right then. I mean, what difference did it make if the guy was faster than I was? Maybe he deserved a break. Maybe he needed a break.

He wiped his eyes with his palms. "I'm sorry, *Julian*."

"No, it's my fault for being nosy—"

"You could not know."

"I shouldn't have asked. It's none of my business."

"Let's talk of happier things."

"Like what?" I said.

His smile got sly. "I think you like Jillian very much."

"What?"

"It is all right," he said. "I will not tell her."

"You can tell her whatever you want—"

"You should ask her to come to the movies with you."

"But I—"

"It will be very nice." He nodded at me, then clammed up. It was like the period at the end of a sentence. He leaned back on the couch and crossed his legs. He'd said his piece.

"Eduardo," I said, "I'm not going to ask Jillian to go to the movies with me."

"Don't you think she's very pretty?"

"It doesn't matter if I do or I don't."

"I don't understand, *Julian*. Didn't you write a letter to her?"

"No."

"No?"

"Well, yes. But it wasn't *my* letter."

"You took someone else's letter?"

"I wrote it. But it's not *from* me."

"Ah, you wrote the letter *for* someone else."

"Please don't tell her."

"But she thinks you wrote it."

I sighed. "Are you sure?"

"*Sí, señor*," he answered.

"But I *told* her—"

"Why would you do such a thing?"

"I don't know. I wish I hadn't."

He shook his head, which annoyed me.

"No, wait," I said. "I *do* know why I did it."

"Why?"

"The same reason you stuck up for Paulo and Hector at Memorial Field."

"But the older boys . . . Paulo and Hector could not defend themselves."

"Well, maybe the person I wrote the letter for couldn't write it himself."

"*Julian,* a woman's heart is very delicate."

"It's a *letter.* Words on a page. Why is it such a big deal?"

"It's more than words on a page," he said. "It is feelings. It is poetry. It is truth. *La verdad.* Do you understand?"

"For God's sake, Eduardo! Why are you blowing it out of proportion?"

"Because love is love."

"How do you know so much about it? How old are you?"

"I am fourteen years old, *Julian.*"

"Shouldn't you be in junior high school?"

"Yes, but I did not speak English very well when *Señor Rifkin* brought me to America. Now I speak it very well. *Very* well. I get *very* good grades. I help Paulo and Hector very much."

"But don't you feel weird about it—I mean, being so much older than the rest of your class?"

"It is where I belong," he said. "I do not feel weird about it."

"But don't you think it's unfair?"

"Unfair how?"

"Look at how big you are," I said. "Plus, you're smart. You should be in eighth grade."

"It would be very difficult, I think—"

"Then at least seventh."

"Thank you, *Julian,* for thinking that I am so smart. But I think I am where I belong."

"You're welcome." I sighed.

"But you do not love Jillian?"

"I *like* Jillian—"

"Perhaps you love her a little?"

"No!"

"Ah."

He ran his right hand across his chin and looked off to the left, deep in thought. I knew I'd made a real mess of things, even if I hadn't meant to. But what could I do? I couldn't unwrite the letter. I felt bad. But also, in a weird way, I felt good. I'd written a love letter, and it had worked—maybe not how it was meant to work, but it had worked. It was like an art project that you thought up and did right. Even if it turned out slightly off, you could still step back and admire the result: the prettiest girl in the entire sixth grade liked me.

But then I remembered Lonnie, how only an hour ago he was talking about marrying Jillian, and now I had to break the news to him that the letter had backfired. I thought about how miserable he was going to be, and I felt low again. Because it wasn't an art project. It was Lonnie's feelings.

"Leave it to me, *Julian*," Eduardo said suddenly.

"Leave what to you?"

"I will tell Jillian what is in your heart."

"You would do that?" I said.

"I know it is not your fault. You meant no harm."

"Do you think she'll be mad?"

He looked at me as if it was a dumb question.

"How mad?" I asked.

"She is a woman, *Julian*."

"And?"

He pointed to his heart. "She lives here."

I had no idea what he meant by that. "Oh."

He winked at me, the same wink as when he was walking off the playground at Memorial Field. Then he turned and walked toward the cellar stairs. I followed him without another word.

I had a new perspective on Jillian's dad when I came out of the cellar. Not that he wasn't a goofball—I mean, he did still have on that MASTER GRILLER apron. Maybe what I had was a new perspective on goofballs. What I mean is, maybe you can't write off a guy just because he happens to be one. Mr. Rifkin had done right by Eduardo, had changed his life, had rescued him from that orphanage and brought him to America. His heart was sure in the right place. Even if it meant I was now the second-fastest kid in P.S. 23.

Lonnie and Jillian, meanwhile, were sitting in lounge chairs by the pool, yakking away. I knew that once he relaxed he would be fine. He was back to being Lonnie, talking a blue streak, and Jillian was cracking up, hanging on his every word. It was good to see. It even occurred to me that maybe, if she spent enough time with him, Jillian would start to like Lonnie. I mean, how could you not? Despite what Amelia said about him, Lonnie's a great guy.

Eduardo peeled off to help Mr. Rifkin with the grill, and I angled straight for Lonnie and Jillian. They didn't even notice me walking up until I was right there—that's what a good time they were having. Then Lonnie caught sight of me and nodded toward the lounge chair to his right. Jillian was to his left, so he was in between us, the center of attention.

"Hey, Jules, I was just telling Jillian about the time you got caught stealing at Lind's Department Store."

"C'mon, Lonnie!"

"It was *hysterical*," he said. "Eric the Red got away with

a G.I. Joe, and Shlomo Shlomo got away with a Dracula model kit, and I had an entire box of baseball cards stashed underneath my shirt—that's like forty packs, four hundred cards—and the three of us hooked up again a block away, and we're standing around, waiting for Julian to come out, and he never made it. We must have stood on that corner for a half hour before it dawned on us that Julian got caught. It didn't seem possible. The guy behind the counter was about a hundred years old, and he was half blind, and even if he noticed what was going on, what could he do? Julian could've dodged him and got to the front door like it was nothing."

Jillian looked past Lonnie to me. "So how did he catch you?"

"I don't know. I guess—"

Lonnie said, "He came out from behind the counter, wagging his finger!"

"I just panicked. I was trying to put back the stuff I took—"

"Tell her what it was!"

"What does that matter?"

"It was a *Gumby*!" Lonnie shouted. That cracked him up again, and it made Jillian laugh too. I could feel my face going red, but I didn't mind, honestly. Lonnie was on a roll. "So Julian's sliding that Gumby back onto the rack, nice and neat, nothing out of place, and meanwhile, the old guy comes up behind him and grabs him by the shoulder—and that's all she wrote. I mean, there are guys who are cut out for crime, and guys who are not cut out for crime. You can figure out what kind of guy Julian is."

"What happened to you?" Jillian asked.

"The old guy called my dad to come pick me up."

"Your dad must've *killed* you!"

"No, that was the weird thing," I said. "I thought he was going to yell, or maybe even take the TV out of my room. But on the drive home he told me in a real calm voice how disappointed he was in me and then let it go. He never mentioned it again. The thing of it was . . . I know how weird this is going to sound. The fact that he didn't make a big deal of it made it worse. It just gave me a bad feeling that lasted for months. I would've rather he yelled."

Jillian leaned forward and lowered her voice. "My dad would have *freaked out* if that happened to me."

"What about your mom?" Lonnie asked. "She seems pretty cool."

That made Jillian grin. "My mom wouldn't have cared. She would've asked what I stole, like whether it was worth it." She took another peek at her mother, then lowered her voice even more. "People always say I look like her, but I think I take after my dad. What do you guys think?"

"You take after both of them," Lonnie said. "You got the best of both worlds."

"What about you, Julian? What do you think?"

I wanted to be careful what I said, given what Eduardo had told me about her feelings. I glanced behind me at Mrs. Rifkin. She'd tied her bikini top and rolled onto her back. But she looked like she had slathered on another layer of suntan oil. You could see the overlapping layers on her belly, the older one that had dried up into a film and the newer one that had more of a shine. I took a good long look at her. "I don't know which one you look more like. Maybe it's both of them, like Lonnie says."

"Do you think my mom has a good body?"

That felt like a wrong question to ask, and I didn't want to answer it, but Jillian was looking straight at me, waiting to hear my opinion. "I guess . . . I mean, for a grown-up."

"Your mom's got a *great* body," Lonnie said.

Eduardo picked that moment to drag over a lounge chair. He sat down on it backward, with his legs straddling the sides and his arms folded across the back. "The food is cooked."

Jillian sat up straight and focused her eyes on him. "Lonnie thinks my mom has a great body. What do you think about that, Eduardo?"

"Your mother is a beautiful woman."

"The neighbors think she's a tease," Jillian said. "They talk about her all the time."

"Hey, if you got it, flaunt it," Lonnie said.

Eduardo nodded in Lonnie's direction without quite going along with what he'd said. "She believes in freedom. It is how she lives."

"But she's my *mom*. It's *so* humiliating."

"You should never be ashamed of your family," Eduardo stated.

Lonnie cracked up. "You wouldn't think so if you met my mom."

"What's wrong with your mom?" Jillian asked.

I knew where the conversation was about to go, and I wanted to tell Lonnie to knock it off, but there was no chance. It happened too fast.

"She doesn't talk right. It's like, '*Thuffering thuccotath.*' I mean, it's not her fault. The Nazis cut her tongue to pieces. But if you listen to her, it's embarrassing. That's the only word for it."

Jillian glared right at him. "That's a *terrible* thing to say!"

The color went out of Lonnie's face. It was pitiful to watch. He was yukking it up one second, and the next second he had a look like that gladiator in *Spartacus* who gets a six-foot spear chucked into his back.

"No, I mean, she's still my mom—"

"How could you say such a thing?" Jillian said.

"It's just that . . . I guess you had to be there. I mean, if you heard her talk . . ."

Jillian looked past him to me. "Have *you* heard her talk, Julian?"

"Sure he has!" Lonnie said. "Lots of times. He'll back me up. Isn't it embarrassing to listen to her talk?"

"It's noticeable, for sure," I managed.

"But is it *embarrassing*?" Jillian asked.

I was grasping for the right answer. "I don't know . . . I'm not sure I'd use that exact word. But the thing is, she's not my mom, so it's hard to say what's embarrassing and what's not embarrassing. But I'd definitely say it's noticeable. Lonnie's right about that."

Right then, Mr. Rifkin walked over with a big plate of hamburgers and hot dogs. He came just in the nick of time. I had no idea what else I was going to say.

"Hey, fellas. What can I do you for?"

"I'll have a hot dog!" I said.

"One dog, coming right up!"

He pushed the plate at me, and I grabbed a hot dog and bun. I didn't even bother to ask for mustard. I just shoved the thing in my mouth and began chewing. That made Jillian crack up, the way I was wolfing it down. Her laughter cut the tension, and things started to feel normal. Awkward, but normal.

Mr. Rifkin passed out hamburgers and hot dogs to Lonnie, Jillian, and Eduardo, so the conversation died down for a couple of minutes. I couldn't remember the last time I was as grateful for silence. Mr. Rifkin went over to sit by his wife. There wasn't much talking between the two of them either, though she did sit up for her burger. Also, he poured her a beer into a plastic cup. He had a beer too, which he drank from the bottle.

Then Eduardo said, out of nowhere, "*Julian*, have you ever played *fútbol*?"

"Do you mean soccer?" I said.

"That is a word only Americans say. The rest of the world says *fútbol*."

"Whatever you call it, I've never played it."

"You should try it," he said. "You are a very fast runner."

Lonnie picked right up on that. "Have you seen this guy run?"

Jillian said, "You never told me you were a runner, Julian."

"He's not just a *runner*," Lonnie said. "He's greased lightning."

Jillian wasn't going to let that slip by. "Well, Eduardo is the fastest runner I've ever seen. He won medals for it in Guatemala. He won trophies for *fútbol* and medals for running. Isn't that right, Eduardo?"

"Then let's have a race!" Lonnie said.

"C'mon, Lonnie!"

Eduardo waved off the idea. "No, *Julian* is much faster."

"There, you see?" Lonnie said. "Even Eduardo knows it. You should have seen him at Track and Field Day last year. The bleachers at Memorial Field were packed. I mean, there must have been two hundred kids jammed in like sardines. The fifth and sixth graders were running forty-yard dashes against each other. Mr. Greetham was timing the winner of each heat with a stopwatch. So he's calling out the times, and it's like five-point-eight, five-point-nine, six-point-one, five-point-nine. You know? It's like that for every heat. Then this Negro kid, Willie, runs a five-point-four. That makes the fifth graders cheer real loud because he's one of them—even though, like I said, Willie is a Negro. But who cares? Five-point-four is still five-point-four. If you're fast, you're fast. So guys are still congratulating Willie, and they don't even notice Julian's heat is about to get started. Except then Greetham yells, 'On your mark . . . get set . . . go!' So they all turn to watch. It's just sick, what happened. Four guys started the race, but three of them quit after about three steps. They stop dead in their tracks because Julian is so far out in front. So Julian finishes the race by himself, not even going full speed, and then Greetham checks his stopwatch, and then he checks it again, and then he says, 'Four-point-nine.' The entire place goes dead quiet. It's like a miracle just happened. But Julian just jogs over to the sideline like it's nothing."

"It's just a number," I said. But I have to admit, listening to Lonnie tell the story like that made me feel real good.

"But that's just a warm-up," Lonnie said. "The guy runs another four-point-nine in the semis and then five-zero in the finals . . . only because he slowed up even more at the end. Willie came in second. It was a sad day for the sixth graders. I know that for a fact because I was one of them. Except I was real proud of Julian, so who cares?"

I don't think Lonnie even realized he'd just told Jillian and Eduardo that he'd been left back, that it was his second time through the sixth grade. I sure wasn't going to point it out to him.

"That is very fast, *Julian*," Eduardo said. "*Very* fast."

Yeah, I was feeling pretty good about myself. I could have listened to them talk like that for hours. Except just when I began to think that maybe I *was* as fast as Lonnie was saying, that maybe I *wasn't* a fake, that maybe the entire school *wasn't* going to find out that I was now the *second*-fastest kid in P.S. 23 on Track and Field Day, Eduardo winked at me. It was that same wink from the playground. It cut right through me. It was as if he was saying, *You and I both know what's going on. We both know the truth. We both know talk is cheap, and that sooner or later we're going to race . . . and we both know how that's going to turn out, don't we?* It was as if he was using Lonnie's bragging on me to get in another dig. That's what it felt like.

Lonnie got real quiet and thoughtful on the bus ride home after the barbecue. The bus was a rattler, even louder than usual, so that made the lack of conversation less noticeable. I felt awful for him. But what could I say? He shouldn't have said what he said about his mom. Even if he didn't mean it in a bad way, which I'm sure he didn't, that's how it came off.

The bus rolled to a stop at a traffic light, and Lonnie looked up at me. He looked tragic. That's the only way to describe the expression on his face. Like his entire life got blown to smithereens. "I should have let well enough alone."

"No, you did all right," I said. "I think she likes you."

"She thinks I'm a bad guy. But I'm *not* a bad guy."

"If she thinks that, then she's off her rocker," I said.

"Do you think it's hopeless?"

"How could it be hopeless? Nothing's hopeless."

"So you think I can fix it?" he said.

"Sure, just be natural the next time you see her."

"Why don't you sit next to her at lunch? Then I'll come over—"

"No way. I'm out of this, Lonnie—"

"C'mon, just sit down next to her in the cafeteria. What's the big deal?"

"She sits with her friends," I said.

"Well, *you're* one of her friends now."

"You're as much her friend as I am. Why don't *you* sit down next to her?"

"I need another chance, Jules. I can't do this alone."

I didn't answer him. That was how we left it.

April 7, 1969

Taking a Break

I know I'm supposed to keep going, or else the deal to get out of English assignments is off. But the barbecue on Saturday got me real emotional, and then writing about it killed Sunday. Just killed it, the entire day. *Sunday.* It was a gorgeous sunny day, warm but not sticky or hot like Saturday, with just the right kind of breeze blowing through the window, and I was holed up inside, scribbling away before I forgot a thing. There's no way I would've spent that much time on a regular paper, not even if I was writing about *Julius Caesar.*

What I'm saying, Mr. Selkirk, is that I deserve a break. There, I said it. I deserve a break. I don't want to write anymore for a while. I don't know how long, exactly. But I need to stop doing this. I'll come back to it sooner or later, but right now I need to give the thing a rest.

Ouch!

It's amazing how taking a break, or just *thinking* about taking a break, gets your juices flowing. I mean, I wasn't going to write another word for the rest of April. But the truth is, I was itching to get going again after only three days. So then I decided I wouldn't write for two weeks. Then that became one week, and now here I am, one week later, sitting down at the desk, Bic in hand, raring to go.

It was a perfect week to take off, as it turned out. Nothing much happened, unless you count what happened to Eric the Red. I don't know if I should even write about it since it's squirmy. But it seemed to get Lonnie's mind off Jillian. He let the entire week pass without nagging me to sit next to her at lunch. Whatever the reason, I needed a break from that too.

The thing with Eric the Red happened Thursday afternoon. I guess I should mention right off that he's all right. He rode in an ambulance to the hospital, sirens blaring, but came home that night. His mom and dad brought him back around nine o'clock. Quentin and I were hanging around in front of the Hampshire House, so we saw them drive up. Eric's dad dropped off him and his mom, then went looking for a parking space, so we got to talk for a couple of minutes. Eric was worn out, but even he was cracking up about it.

I mean, it *was* kind of hilarious. Not at the time, of course, but afterward, once we knew for sure that Eric didn't get killed. The six of us were out back in Ponzini—Howie Wartnose, Shlomo Shlomo, Quentin, Eric, Lonnie, and me. It felt good to be there with the entire gang. It seemed like weeks since all six of us showed up at once. Also, I knew Lonnie would be his regular self. He never talks about Jillian to the rest of them.

He *was* his regular self too. It was as though he'd been saving up the real Lonnie, keeping him under wraps, but now, back in Ponzini, surrounded by the entire gang, he let loose. He was on us from the second we got there. It was brutal how he was ranking us out, but it was beautiful. It was art, almost. He had us cracking up at one another and at ourselves. It wasn't *what* he said. If I quoted him word for word, you'd just shrug it off. But the thing about Lonnie is, when he's his regular self, *what* he says doesn't mean as much as *how* he says it.

So the six of us, like I said, were out back in Ponzini, and Lonnie was ranking on us, and just when it felt as though he was going to run out of insults, out of nowhere Eric decided he wanted to walk Ponzini's Fence. Why he picked that moment, I have no idea. But he asked Lonnie to bring him the circus axle, and right off Lonnie went and got it for him.

Now I guess I should explain about the circus axle. It's actually a car axle that fell out of the bottom of one of the rusted-out wrecks in Ponzini a couple of years ago. Lonnie was the one who first noticed it and dragged it out from underneath the car. It's maybe four feet long, solid metal, and heavier than you'd think. We call it the circus axle because we use it to balance ourselves when we walk the fence that separates Ponzini from the private backyards on the other side. It's like a circus act. The fence is about sixty feet long and six feet high, and it takes nerve to walk the entire length because there's nothing but concrete on the Ponzini side and cobblestone patios on the other.

The idea to use the circus axle to walk the fence was Lonnie's, but the first guy to climb up and do it was Quick Quentin. Lonnie dared him, and Quentin did it like it was nothing. Once I saw Quentin do it, then I had to do it, and then Lonnie did it himself. Howie Wartnose was going to go next, but then Victor Ponzini showed up—he must have been watching us from his bedroom window—and begged us to let him try it, so we did.

He got about two steps, dropped the axle, then keeled to the left and fell off. He landed flat on his stomach, then rolled onto his back, gasping for air. He kept mouthing a word that we couldn't make out. There was no sound, just his mouth widening and tightening. You know that thing a fish does when it gets yanked out of water? That's what his mouth looked like. But then Ponzini managed to suck in enough air to form the word: "Wind . . ." We leaned in closer. "Wind . . . wind . . . wind . . ." That was when we figured out what he meant. He'd gotten the wind knocked out of him. That cracked us up for some reason. Of course, it was mean to laugh while he was still lying on the ground. But the way he was gasping the word "wind" just seemed real comical. Maybe you had to be there.

After that, Lonnie began to call the fence Ponzini's Fence, which is how the lot came to be called Ponzini. It doesn't quite make sense, if you stop and think about it, but for whatever reason, the name stuck.

Victor Ponzini was the first person to fall off the fence but not the last. It took Howie Wartnose three times to make it across, and he got scraped up pretty good the first two tries. Shlomo Shlomo lost his balance, dropped the axle, and tried to jump down—except the axle hit the fence, seesawed back up, and hit Shlomo in the chin as he was jumping down. The poor guy wound up with three stitches and a tetanus shot. He never tried again after that. Beverly Segal fell off, but then she tried again a couple of weeks later and became the first and only girl to walk the entire fence.

I think it was watching Beverly Segal walk the fence that made Eric feel as if he had to do it too. He was the only one of us who'd never tried. But the thing was, he had a real phobia about it. He didn't even like to *hop* the fence, which we had to do from time to time to get back a ball during stickball. Even Lonnie laid off him about it. I mean, you don't want to force a guy to do what he can't do.

But for whatever reason, Eric stepped up last Thursday and asked Lonnie for the circus axle. Maybe we should've tried to talk him out of it. But how can you talk the guy out of it without making him feel worse? Put yourself in Eric's place. I mean, *Beverly Segal did it.* If you're Eric, even if you fall flat on your face, I think you have to give it a shot.

So Lonnie went and got the axle while the rest of us helped Eric climb the fence. You could feel how scared he was going up. I had hold of his left leg, right below the knee, and I could feel the tremble running down his calf. I didn't think he was going to be able to stand, but when Lonnie held out the circus axle, he grabbed the end of it and used the leverage to hoist himself upright. I still had hold of his left sneaker, which was as high as I could reach, and Quentin still had hold of his right sneaker, but at that point there was nothing we could have done if he lost his balance.

Eric nodded at Lonnie to let go of the circus axle, and then he pulled it up to his hips, into balanced position, and then Quentin and I let go of his sneakers . . . and Eric was on his own. It took him a couple of seconds to gather himself, but he got the hang of it pretty fast, letting the axle drift up and down instead of adjusting with his hips. That's the trick. If you feel yourself tilting to one side, you lift the axle on that side until you come upright again.

The worst thing you can do, of course, is panic. To be honest, that's what I thought was going to happen to Eric. I was afraid that he'd built the thing up so much in his mind that he wouldn't trust his feet. The fence doesn't move. When you stop and think about it, walking the fence is just like walking a straight line—except you're six feet up in the air. If you put one foot in front of the other, and you do it again and again, there's nothing to it.

So how do you *not* panic? You don't look down. That seems like common sense, but it's the difference between guys who make it across and guys who don't. If you keep your eyes straight ahead and let the circus axle do the work for you, you've got it made. But if you look down, and you start smiling at your friends, and you start thinking about how their eyes are on you, thinking about how spastic you're going to look if you fall, thinking about which side to jump down if you feel yourself falling—then you're dead meat.

That's what got Eric the Red. Looking down, I mean. He was doing fine for the first ten steps, working the axle like a pro, but then Quentin and Howie started yelling at him, telling him he was halfway across, which wasn't true, and he knew it wasn't true, which made him glance down to give them a sarcastic look. Then Lonnie shushed all of us and told Eric to focus on what he was doing, which was good advice, but *that* made him nod down at Lonnie, then look forward, then shake his head, then look forward . . . and that was the beginning of the end. His knees began to wobble, first the right and then the left. He recovered for a split second, but then his hips started to go. By then, his eyes were bulging out of their sockets. Full panic. He let go of the circus axle, which clanged down on the fence and then clattered to the ground. His arms were flailing in circles.

"Jump down!" Lonnie yelled.

It was more good advice. The trouble was that Eric was keeling to the right at that moment. The natural thing for him to do would have been to jump in that direction, but that would have landed him in one of the private backyards. The rest of us were standing in Ponzini, to his left, so Eric took it in his mind to jump back toward us.

He split the difference.

He came straight down on the bar at the top of the fence, with one leg on either side. Right on his crotch. You could hear the air go out of him, a long, loud *"Ooooooomph."* For a second, no one moved. Not even Eric. His eyes were shut, his hands gripping the top of the fence. Then he opened his eyes, turned his head to the right, and puked. It was disgusting to watch, but he puked his guts into one of the private backyards.

Afterward, his head sank down onto his chest. His eyes were still open, and he was still holding on to the bar at the top of the fence, but he was out. You could see the glaze over his eyes. There was no one home. He started to roll to the right, away from us, but Lonnie lunged forward and grabbed his left leg. Quentin and I jumped up onto the fence and caught him by the waist. The three of us managed to ease him down from the fence on the Ponzini side.

We laid him on the ground and huddled around him. After half a minute, he came back behind his eyes. He knew where he was and what had happened. He curled up like a baby, with his hands over his crotch, and began to moan. He had tears in his eyes, but how could you hold that against him? It wasn't like he was bawling. It was more like the tears were being squeezed out of him.

"You're going to be all right," Lonnie whispered to him.

But then Eric opened his mouth, and it was full of blood.

That made us step back.

Howie tugged on Lonnie's sleeve. "He's not all right."

Lonnie turned to me, and I knew the drill from when Quentin lost his eyebrows. I sprinted home and yelled to my mom to call an ambulance. She started to ask questions, but I cut her off and just said, "Eric got hurt." That got her attention. I almost told her to send the ambulance to Ponzini, but then I remembered that the name would mean nothing to her or to the ambulance driver, so I gave her the street address on Parsons Boulevard and told her we were in the vacant lot behind the building. She said she'd be there right after she called for help.

I ran back outside.

Eric was sitting upright by the time I got back to Ponzini. He wasn't doing it on his own, though. Shlomo and Howie were holding his shoulders, and Quentin and Lonnie were talking to him. There was still a lot of blood around his lips and on his chin.

"The ambulance is on its way," I called to them.

Lonnie turned to me as I knelt down next to him. "I don't think it's too bad. I think maybe he just bit his tongue."

Eric didn't react to what Lonnie said. He wasn't listening at that point.

"You don't think it's his balls?" Shlomo said.

Lonnie said, "I've never seen a guy fall like that. It could be his balls. It could be his balls got knocked up into his mouth. I'm not sure. How long till the ambulance gets here?"

Just then, we heard a siren. It was coming down Parsons Boulevard. Another five minutes passed before the doctors figured out how to get through the building and back to Ponzini. Then, at last, two of them rushed through the rear exit of the parking garage. My mom was right behind them—which kind of embarrassed me. But what could I do? Tell her not to come?

Right off, the doctors made Eric lie back down. He was still too woozy to answer their questions, so Lonnie told them what had happened. The doctors kind of smiled at one another when he explained how Eric fell. I didn't like that much. It seemed kind of unprofessional, in my opinion. Then one of the doctors stood up and walked back out to the ambulance. It was a relief, in a weird way, the fact that he didn't seem in too big a rush. He returned a couple of minutes later with a canvas stretcher. They lifted Eric onto it and hauled him out of Ponzini. We followed them through the parking garage and watched them load him into the back of the ambulance. He was starting to come around by then. We heard him telling the doctors his phone number. One of the doctors climbed into the back of the ambulance after him while the other climbed behind the wheel to drive. The siren started to blare. Then the back door of the ambulance slammed shut from the inside. That was the last we saw of Eric till he came home that night.

It turned out that there wasn't much wrong with him. He just got bruised real bad where you don't want to get bruised. Plus, he *had* bitten his tongue like Lonnie said. We were thankful that he was all right. But believe me, I'd hate to be Eric the Red from now on. He's never going to hear the end of it.

The Truth Comes Out

I'll be the first to admit it: I don't understand girls. Plus, out of all the girls I've ever met, I understand Jillian the least. I mean, it made sense that she wanted nothing to do with me after the barbecue. I figured Eduardo must have had his talk with her, and she was real upset, so she'd decided to avoid me. *That* made sense. But then, this afternoon, she waltzed up to my table as I sat down for lunch in the cafeteria. There I was, saving seats for Lonnie and the rest of the gang, and I looked up, and she was standing right next to me, carrying her lunch tray, smiling as though nothing had happened.

"Mind if I sit down, Julian?"

"The guys will be here in a few minutes."

"I'll move when they come."

"All right, but it might be kind of weird."

She set her tray down on the table and slid in next to me on the bench. "Are you mad at me, Julian?"

The question stunned me. "Why would *I* be mad at *you*?"

"You didn't talk to me last week."

"You didn't talk to me either," I said.

"I didn't talk to you because you didn't talk to me."

"I didn't *not* talk to you."

"You didn't even smile at me," she said. "Did I do something wrong?"

"I didn't mean not to smile at you. I guess I just had stuff on my mind."

"What kind of stuff?"

"Just stuff. Nothing special."

"The girls in class think you're *so* smart."

"I'm not *so* smart," I said. "I'm just maybe regular smart."

"That's not what Mr. Selkirk says."

"What does he have to do with it?"

"He thinks you're *real* smart."

"Did you read his mind?"

"Why else would he let you get out of the final paper on *Julius Caesar*?"

"How did you find out?" I said.

"Word gets around, Julian. He thinks you're writing a book."

"I'm not writing a *book*."

"He thinks you are," she said. "He thinks you've caught the 'writing bug.'"

"That's just stupid."

"Why is it stupid?"

"There's no such thing as the 'writing bug.' Plus, anyway, how do you know what Selkirk thinks?"

"Because I asked him if *I* could write a book to get out of *Julius Caesar*, and he said no. When I said that wasn't fair, he said that writing was your thing. So then I said maybe writing was my thing too. But he shook his head. He told me he thought you were going to be a famous author. Those were his exact words. I swear on my mother's life."

"Well, what does he know?"

"He said you've got the writing bug bad."

(I don't know why you said that to her, Mr. Selkirk. Plus, I don't know why you think that. Because, in my opinion, there's no such thing as the writing bug, and even if there is, I don't have it. That's the truth. If you don't believe me, listen to what I said next.)

"Writing doesn't mean squat to me," I said. "I could stop doing it tomorrow. I'm *going* to stop doing it at the end of June. You think I'm going anywhere near a composition book over the summer?"

"I'm just telling you what he told me," she said.

146

I stared down at the table and shook my head.

"So you're not mad at me?"

"No, not at all," I said.

That was when it happened: she leaned forward and kissed me on the cheek.

I must've given her the weirdest look ever. "Why did you do that?"

"You said you weren't mad at me. Are you mad at me now?"

"No, but why did you do it?"

"Because I wanted to do it."

"That's it?" I said. "You wanted to do it, so you just did it?"

"I didn't think you'd mind."

"I don't *mind*—"

Right then, Eric, Howie, and Shlomo showed up at the table with their lunch trays. I was afraid for a split second that they'd seen what had just happened, but they were too busy yakking it up even to notice Jillian was sitting next to me. They just slid down in their usual places without missing a beat. Quentin and Lonnie were a couple of steps behind them. Lonnie, of course, noticed Jillian right off. His face was red as a tomato, then, a second later, pale as a sheet.

As he was about to sit down, Jillian stood up. "I guess I'll get going."

That caught their attention. They glanced up but none of them spoke.

To break the tension, I introduced her. I said, "Guys, this is Jillian."

Quentin was the only one who managed to squeeze out an actual "Hi."

I turned to Jillian. "These are the guys. . . . You already know Lonnie."

"Hi, Lonnie," she said. She nodded in a general way and walked off.

The second she was out of earshot, Shlomo let out a wolf whistle. That cracked up the rest of them, except for Lonnie. He sat there stone-faced, probably still shaking off the shock of finding her there.

Then Howie said, "Is that your new *girlfriend*, Julian?"

"What? No!"

"Then who is she?"

"She's just a girl from my class. That's all."

"Then how come she was sitting so close to you?"

"She had a question about English," I said.

Shlomo said, "All right, but don't let it happen again. She might give Eric a boner. In his condition, that could be fatal."

That cracked us up again and got us back to normal. Except for Lonnie, that is. I snuck a glance at him, and he still looked stunned. Which was real ironical since he was the one who wanted *me* to sit at *Jillian's* table. Here he'd had a perfect chance to ask her to stick around, to eat lunch with us, and he couldn't get out a single word. I figured at least he had let go of that idea. So maybe, as awkward as it was, something good would come out of it.

On the other hand, the fact that she had showed up at our table in the first place made no sense. Why would she do that after Eduardo had talked to her? Unless, of course, he'd chickened out and hadn't talked to her. That didn't seem likely, given what I knew of him. But the only way to find out for sure was to track him down after school. So that's what I did.

As soon as school let out, I went looking for Eduardo at the playground at Memorial Field, and that's right where I found him. I mean, that guy loved to play tag. He wasn't hard to notice in a wild scramble of about a dozen fifth graders, including Paulo and Hector. There might even have been one or two fourth graders in the group. I was ashamed to be seen in the vicinity, to tell the truth. But what choice did I have? I waited at the edge of the playground and waved a couple of times until Eduardo caught sight of me.

He waved at me. "*Julian*, come join us!"

"I need to ask you something!" I yelled back.

He called time-out, then jogged over. "What is it, my friend?"

"I talked to Jillian today."

"Yes."

"She acted kind of weird."

"Yes."

"It's just that . . . did you talk to her?"

He gave me a sly grin. "About what?"

"You know."

"I'm not sure what you mean, *Julian*."

"What you and I talked about in your room."

"Ah. Yes."

"So you *did* talk to her about it?"

"No, *señor*."

That made me gasp. "Why not?"

"*Julian*, you are so young. . . ."

"You *said* you'd talk to her. I trusted you."

"Trust love, *Julian*."

"You *lied* to me."

"I lied *for* you."

"What does that even mean?"

Eduardo smiled down at me and tapped me on my left shoulder. He looked me straight in the eye in a real serious way. "Do you know what *that* means, *Julian*?"

"What?"

He turned and sprinted off. After he had run a good distance, he spun around and called back to me, "It means . . . *Tag, you're it!*"

You know that saying about seeing red? Until that moment, I thought it was just a saying. But right then, for the first time, it made perfect sense to me. It wasn't so much that I saw the *color* red. What I saw was heat. Or rather, I *felt* heat behind my eyes, which made the world look reddish. The benches, the swings, the faces of the fourth and fifth graders looked reddish. Even the air looked reddish. The reddest thing of all was Eduardo. He looked as if he was glowing red, like a cinnamon gumdrop. He was waving at me, daring me to chase him, grinning the entire time. That grin . . . that was the reddest thing of the reddest thing. It set every nerve in my body on edge.

Without even thinking about it, I charged after him. I didn't just want to tag him. I wanted to tag him so hard I'd shove him to the ground. He turned and started to run, but I closed on him real fast. Too fast, as it turned out. Just as I put out my hand, he veered hard right, and I shot past him.

"*¡Olé!*" he yelled.

When I turned to face him again, there was that grin. That was what I saw. Nothing else. I put my head down and rushed him a second time. I could hear his footsteps in front of me, dancing left and right. But at the last second, there was no sound. I looked up, and I was past him again. I don't know whether he'd faked right or left, but I had missed him, and he was still standing in the same place. He hadn't moved a foot in either direction.

"¡Olé, Julian!"

That was when I heard the laughter. Fourth and fifth graders were laughing at me.

"Hey, *toro!*" Eduardo called.

"What?"

"*¡Toro! ¡Toro!*"

For a third time, I sprinted after him. Except this time, I kept my head up. He took off but let me get real close, swiveling his hips side to side. I was inches from him, not even a fingertip away, but when I leaned forward, he veered just out of reach.

It was too much to take, getting that close. I lunged just as he broke hard right. I tried to cut back with him, but my feet got tangled, and I started to fall. When I say I *started* to fall, what I mean is it wasn't the kind of fall that happens at once. That fall had a story—a beginning, a middle, and an end. It was me against gravity. I thought I might right myself, get back my balance, except I was too far gone. It took me nine full steps to fall, and I was fighting it the entire time. But after the ninth step, I surrendered. I put out my hands and tumbled forward. I rolled with it, head over heels, skinning both of my palms, but given how hard I was running, it could have been worse. I ended up sitting on the ground, staring at my palms.

Not a second passed before I heard Eduardo standing above me saying, "Are you hurt, *Julian?*"

I didn't even look up at him. "I'm fine!"

That brought another wave of laughter from the fourth and fifth graders.

"Are you sure?"

"I said I'm *fine!*"

I jumped up . . . or at least, I tried to. What I didn't realize was that the fall had landed me under the first row of monkey bars. As I jumped up, I clanged my head against an iron bar. I heard the *clang* inside and outside my head at the same time, even before I felt the pain.

The next thing I knew, I was rolling on the ground, clutching my skull, moaning like I'd been shot. It was pure instinct. It wasn't as if I'd decided to roll around or grab my head or moan. There was no decision involved. I felt Eduardo trying to hold me still. But I kept twisting and squirming. Then, at last, he got a grip on me. He forced my shoulders to the ground.

"¡Julian! ¡Julian!"

My head was pulsing with pain, and I could still hear ringing in my ears. But the worst of it was that I could feel tears rolling down my cheeks. I was crying . . . *in front of fourth and fifth graders.* The shame of it washed over me. If I hadn't been crying already, the shame would have made me cry.

"Open your eyes, *Julian.* Say if you can see me."

It was the last thing I wanted to do, but I slowly

opened my eyes. Through the tears, I saw him. He had a strange, stretched-out look on his face. I realized at once he was crying too.

"Say how many fingers I have up, *Julian*."

He held up three fingers on his right hand.

As bad as I felt, that cracked me up. It seemed like such a dumb, pointless thing to ask. I squinted at him and said, "Six."

Then I smiled. It hurt like crazy to smile, but I couldn't help myself.

That made Eduardo start to laugh. "You have a hard head, *Julian*."

He put out his hand, and I took it to sit up. Now here's the weird part, or at least, the part that made the least sense. As much as my head hurt, which was a lot, what I felt at that moment was mostly relief. The truth had come out: I was no longer the fastest kid in P.S. 23. Fourth graders and fifth graders knew it, which meant that sixth graders were sure to find out about it. There was nothing I could do or say to keep it a secret. So I nodded. I wasn't sure whether I was only nodding to myself or whether my head was actually moving up and down, but either way, I had accepted the truth. Sitting there on the ground, under the monkey bars, I had accepted the fact that I was now the *second*-fastest kid in P.S. 23.

April 26, 1969

Buddying Up with Beverly Segal

Here's the question I've asked myself over and over since last week: Why should I care about being the fastest kid in P.S. 23? I *do* care. Don't get me wrong. But why *should* I? It's not like the school is the world. Which means that even if I were still the fastest kid in P.S. 23, or even in District 25, or in the borough of Queens, or in the entire city of New York, that would still leave an awful lot of the world unaccounted for. No matter how fast I got, there would always be some guy somewhere who was faster. Lots of guys, if you think about it. I mean, think about those guys in the Olympics. Even the guy who finished dead last in the hundred-yard dash would blow Eduardo right off the track.

What I've figured out, in other words, is you've got

to be philosophical about stuff. Maybe that's not what you *wanted* me to figure out, Mr. Selkirk, because it's got nothing to do with Danley Dimmel. But maybe it's even more important. I know I wrote some mean things last week . . . like when I said the only reason I've kept this thing going was to get out of doing the Shakespeare assignment. I guess I was mad that you were talking to Jillian about me. But writing down my thoughts has made me into a more philosophical person. Really and truly it has. So I guess what I'm saying is that I'm sorry for what I said. Maybe I don't have the "writing bug," but I *do* like writing.

Anyway, news traveled fast about the fall I took running after Eduardo and about how I couldn't catch him. I don't think Eduardo said a word himself, but that kind of thing is like dynamite to fourth and fifth graders. It rattles their universe, like waking up one morning and watching the sun rising in the west instead of the east, or like finding out there's another number between twelve and thirteen. They thought that Julian Twerski was the fastest kid in their school, and then they saw the ugly truth firsthand. It must've thrown them for a loop.

Around the block, the only guy who ragged me was Shlomo Shlomo . . . and with him the ragging wasn't so much about what happened in the playground but about the fact that he'd been the first one to tell me how fast

Eduardo was. He kept after me with, "Didn't I *tell* you? I *told* you! Maybe from now on you'll *listen* when I *tell* you stuff." Eric the Red shrugged at the news, then muttered under his breath, "Well, at least you didn't get your balls crushed." Howie Wartnose patted me on the shoulder and let it go at that. Quick Quentin said that it wasn't a big deal, that I was still the fastest guy on the block, and that was what mattered to him.

The only guy with no reaction whatsoever was Lonnie. Which kind of confused me at first, but then made sense the more I thought about it. He and I are so close that the news must have hit him real hard. He must've felt like he was the one who'd taken that nine-step fall. When I remembered how he'd been bragging on me at Jillian's barbecue, I realized how much I'd let him down.

Meanwhile, life goes on. Friday was the class trip to the Metropolitan Museum. That's not the kind of thing I go for—I mean, class trips are fine until about third grade. But as you get older, class trips can be kind of humiliating. It would be one thing if your teacher just sent you out and told you to meet up at the museum. But instead you get herded like sheep into the school bus, and then you get that long serious talk about how scary Manhattan is, and how if a stranger starts talking to you, you're supposed to scream your lungs out. Then you're dropped off at the museum steps, and you have to do that stupid count-off just to make sure no one jumped out of the bus at the last tollbooth.

I mean, we're *sixth graders!*

As for the museum itself, I've got nothing against it. I like art as much as the next guy. Maybe not as much as Amelia likes art, but I like it. Not the kind of art where the guide needs to explain it to you, where he's got to tell you what it is and why it's good. There's lots of junk in the museum that's there only because it's old, and because it came from ancient Greece. I mean, so what? Junk is junk. I don't need to hear a guy in a blue uniform going on and on about a miniature statue with a broken-off head, about what it's supposed to represent and what it says about life in ancient Athens. For all he knows, it could've been some Greek kid's Gumby.

What I like are big paintings, the kind that take up an entire wall. I also like when the stuff in the painting looks exactly like the stuff in real life, so it's like a photograph—except it came from the painter's brain instead of from the world. It's creepy to think of it that way. You're looking into the mind of a guy who's been dead for centuries, and you're feeling what he was feeling, or at least what he wanted you to feel, noticing how good he was at what he was doing when he was alive. It's creepy because it reminds you that sooner or later you're going to die, that whatever you're good at now won't matter because you'll be dead and gone and no one will care . . . unless, of course, you're a painter, in which case, if you luck out, maybe a class of sixth graders will walk past your painting and think about you.

One painting I liked a lot at the Metropolitan Museum was by an Italian guy named Caravaggio, who lived from 1571 to 1610. It's called *Judith Beheading Holofernes.* That thing is just gruesome. It shows an Israelite woman cutting off the head of an Assyrian general. Now, when I say the painting shows her cutting off the guy's head, I mean it *shows* her doing it, right down to the gushing blood as she saws through his neck. But the worst thing is the expression on Holofernes's face. *He knows what's happening.* His mouth is wide open, and his eyes are bugging out, and the knife is halfway into his neck, and he can feel it going through him. Meanwhile, Judith is holding him by the hair, taking her time, sizing up the job, calm as can be, going about her business. I'm telling you, if you saw something like that happen in a movie, you'd run out of the theater screaming your head off . . . which, I guess, means you'd wind up like Holofernes.

(I hope that counts as the museum writing assign-ment, Mr. Selkirk.)

I started the trip buddied up with Freddie Nalvin, but once we got to the museum there was a lot of trading off, so I wound up with Beverly Segal—who's in the other class that made the trip. It wasn't personal. Freddie carries around a handkerchief because his palms sweat a lot, but he's a good guy, and it wasn't like we were going to hold hands. But Beverly was desperate to switch because she started out with Hank Feltscher, who's as crazy about her as Howie Wartnose is. About half the guys in the sixth grade are stuck on Beverly, to be honest. It's hard to think of her that way since she and I grew up together. She's not the prettiest girl around, but she's got a nice face with soft eyes and a big smile. Plus, she'll *do* stuff. She's always up for a game of Ringolevio or Johnny on the Pony. Most girls won't get involved because of the tackling and sweating. But Beverly will jump right in and mix it up. If there were such a thing as Track and Field Day for girls, she'd come in first for sure.

That's why the other girls *hate* her. You should hear the rumors that follow her around. There's one about how she went behind the bushes at Memorial Field with Howie Wartnose—which is a total joke, if you know the two of them. I think Howie would drop dead of a heart attack if he ever went behind the bushes with Beverly Segal. You'd have to bury him right there, behind the bushes. He'd die with a stupid grin on his face, though. That's for sure.

But here's the thing. If you get to know her, Beverly's fun to talk to. I don't think I was bored for one minute, and it wasn't because of the art. She and I were shooting the breeze the entire time, walking from room to room, taking in paintings and sculptures, but also arguing about sports, about whether Bobby Murcer could get a hit against Tom Seaver, about whether Joe Namath could throw a football farther than Johnny Unitas . . . and meanwhile, we were paying no attention to the poor museum guide.

The three hours just zoomed by.

The one thing that was awkward, buddied up with Beverly, was strolling past nude statues. I'm sure it would've felt awkward even with Freddie Nalvin, but two guys can at least laugh about it. With a girl, you don't know how that's going to go over, whether it will make matters worse. Beverly must have been thinking the same thing because after about the sixth statue, she turned to me and said, "So I guess underwear wasn't invented until later."

That cut the tension, and I was grateful.

By the time the trip was over and we'd shuffled back onto the buses, I was looking at Beverly Segal in a different light. I could kind of understand why Howie Wartnose was so nuts about her. She was the kind of girl who made you forget that she was a girl. You could just talk to her, and she would come back with answers that made sense. She said what she meant. You didn't have to figure the angles with her. She was just a good sort.

May 2, 1969

Betrayals

You know the old saying "No good deed goes unrewarded"? My dad has a different saying: "No good deed goes unpunished." What he means is that doing a favor for another person *should* bring you good luck, or at least get you a favor in return, but that's not how life works. The favor I did for Beverly Segal is a perfect example. She wanted to get rid of Hank Feltscher, so I traded buddies and spent the entire museum trip with her. If that doesn't count as a good deed, I don't know what does. Except now it turns out Howie Wartnose is mad at me because he thinks I've got a thing for Beverly Segal. Which isn't true. He should be grateful that I got between Hank Feltscher and Beverly since Hank Feltscher actually *does* have a thing for her. That would be the *logical* way to look at it. But that's not how Howie Wartnose looks at it.

So now Howie won't sit at our table in the cafeteria if I'm there. To be honest, I didn't even realize there was a problem the first couple of times . . . until Quentin clued me in. After that, I tried to make things right. I tried to talk to Howie after school, but he turned his back and kept walking.

I'm not too worried about it, though, because Lonnie's on the case. He sat next to Howie on the bus every morning for the entire week, and the two of them were talking a mile a minute. Lonnie can be real persuasive, so I'm sure Howie will come around.

But that's not the only grief I got about buddying up with Beverly. Monday morning, before I even knew what was going on with Howie Wartnose, I walked into homeroom and found Jillian sitting at my desk. She had her hands folded together on the desktop in a real sarcastic way, like she was still in second grade. She was also smiling a fake smile.

She looked up at me when I came over, but she didn't move from my seat. "How was your weekend, Julian?"

"It was all right. How was yours?"

"Just fine."

"You're sitting at my desk."

"Oh, am I?"

"What's wrong?" I said.

"What could be wrong, Julian?"

"Well, you're sitting at my desk. I don't mind, but it doesn't seem right."

"I wanted to see the world the way you see it."

"I don't think sitting at my desk is going to—"

"No, it's working," she said. "Now I see things the way you see them."

"What do you mean?"

"Now I see how beautiful Beverly Segal is."

"You think I think Beverly Segal is beautiful?"

"Why else would you buddy up with her?"

"Beverly is from the block. She and I have been friends for years."

That was when Jillian's eyes welled up. "So she's your girlfriend?"

"No, she's not my girlfriend!"

She brushed away her tears with the palms of her hands, then said in a low voice, almost a whisper, "Why do you hate me, Julian? I don't understand. What did I do wrong?"

I glanced from side to side as she spoke. The room was still filling up. There were about a dozen conversations going on, so no one was paying attention to Jillian and me. But that wasn't going to last much longer.

"You didn't do a thing wrong," I said.

"Then why don't you like me anymore?"

"Anymore?"

"Lots of guys think *I'm* beautiful," she said.

"I don't like *anyone*, Jillian."

"But you wrote me a love letter," she said.

"I told you—the letter wasn't from me."

"But it sounds like you. I can hear your voice. I can hear your *heart*."

"Maybe I helped to write it—"

She looked up at me hopefully.

"Here's the thing, Jillian. If I were going to write a letter like that for myself, you're the one I'd write it to for sure. I think you're real pretty, and I also think you're real smart. So maybe, when I was helping to write it, I got carried away. But the letter isn't mine. It's not *from* me. It wasn't my idea."

"But it was your words?"

"Yes," I said.

"And your feelings too?"

"Look," I said, "if I tell you the truth, do you swear to keep it between us?"

"Of course I do!"

"Do you swear?"

She looked me dead in the eyes. "I would *never* tell your secrets, Julian."

I inhaled. "You know my friend Lonnie?"

"Sure, the one who came to my barbecue."

"Yeah. He's a great guy."

She half shrugged and brushed away a tear. "He's all right, I guess."

"He's not just all right. He's a *great* guy. He's smarter than anyone I know. Maybe it doesn't always show in school, but once you get to know him, you realize how smart he is. I mean, he's just an all-around great guy."

She got a sudden look on her face, like she'd just figured things out. "Did Lonnie tell you not to like me anymore?"

"What?"

"I got mad at him when he was talking about his mother. Did I hurt his feelings? I didn't mean to do it. I don't mind apologizing if I hurt his feelings. It's just that . . . how could you talk about your mother that way?"

"First of all, Lonnie loves his mother—"

"I'll tell him I'm sorry. I don't mind."

"That's just his way of joking around."

"I want to be friends with your friends."

"Second of all, Lonnie's not just my friend. He's my *best* friend. He's the greatest guy I know. It's not just me who thinks that. You could ask any guy on Thirty-Fourth Avenue who the greatest guy he knows is, and the answer will come up the same every time. It's Lonnie."

"I know you're loyal to your friends, Julian. I'll apologize to Lonnie the next time I see him."

I felt defeat wash over me. "Jillian, it was *Lonnie's* letter."

She lurched back and put her hand over her mouth.

"I wrote it for him. But only because he asked me to do it."

"How *could* you, Julian?" Tears flooded back to her eyes.

"I thought it was a bad idea. That's the honest truth. But I did it because Lonnie is a great guy, and I knew he would do it for me."

"Why would you need Lonnie to write a letter for you?"

"I wouldn't," I said. "But let's say I needed to drag a couch down the street—"

"*What?*"

"I know it's a bad example. But let's say I did—"

She let out a loud sob. The entire class turned toward us. It was like that scene in the movie *Children of the Damned* where the kids' heads spin around all at once. Jillian lowered her face into her hands and cried, and I stood next to her, with my hands in my pockets, waiting for her to get up out of my seat.

After several seconds, I whispered, "I'm sorry."

"It's all right, Julian," she managed to answer.

"I like you a lot."

"You don't have to say that."

"No, it's the truth," I said. "If Lonnie hadn't thought of it first, I would've written the letter myself."

She looked up at me. "Really?"

"I mean, I can't say for sure—"

"But you do like me a lot."

"Yes, but so does Lonnie. He's *crazy* about you. If you just got to know him—"

She stood up and wiped the tears from her eyes. "All right, I understand, Julian."

The way she said that sent a chill through me. But there was no way to continue the conversation. She walked back to her desk, and I slid in behind mine. I kept my head down until I could feel the rest of the kids lose interest. They went back to their conversations. Five minutes later, the morning bell rang, and class started.

May 9, 1969

When They Get Started . . .

You know that short story we read the other day, "My Old Man" by Ernest Hemingway? I didn't think too much of it at the time. It seemed like one of those stories that goes on and on and then stops, and afterward you wonder why you had to read it in the first place. It's sad, I guess, how the kid's dad gets knocked off the racehorse and killed, and then the horse has to be killed too. Actually, now that I'm writing about it, it's *real* sad—even if the kid's dad was a crook. I mean, no kid should have to see his dad get killed. It kind of choked me up just now, thinking back on it. (Don't worry, I'm not going to bawl.) But what stuck in my head was the last line: "Seems like when they get started they don't leave a guy nothing."

That's just how I feel after last week.

First came a note from Lonnie, which Quentin handed to me at the bus stop on Tuesday morning.

Dear Julian,
    I know I don't write so good as you and I might make mistakes with where commas and punctuations go and such. But I'm writing to say I saw you kissing with Jillian last week in the cafeteria but I tried to act like it was nothing but yesterday she said you told her to tell me she liked you and not me. I think that stinks Julian. I trusted you because you were my friend but you stabbed me right in the back like it was nothing. I ought to punch you but I won't on account of how long we were friends but I don't want to talk to you no more from now on.
                    Sincerely, your x-friend Lonnie

Lonnie's note, like I said, came on Tuesday morning, and it just tore me up. Looking back, though, things went downhill from there. I could have handled the note by itself. I'm sure if nothing else had happened, Lonnie and I would've talked things out. The thing about Lonnie is that he's fair, and the truth was that he had no reason to be mad at me.

That's what I was going to tell him after school on Tuesday. It had to be after school because I couldn't walk up to him in the cafeteria, when the rest of the guys were around. No one besides me knew how he felt about Jillian, and I wanted to respect his privacy. So I waited until after school—I figured Lonnie would be as torn up as I was about what had happened, and I knew that when he felt like that, he liked to walk home by himself.

I let him have a five-minute head start, and then I ran a couple of blocks until he came into sight. He was walking up 149th Street, about to turn the corner at Bayside Avenue. I jogged up behind him. His shoulders were hunched forward. He looked wrecked and miserable even from behind, which was just what I expected. He turned when he heard my footsteps.

"Wait up!" I called to him.

He stopped and shook his head. The look on his face was more sad than mad.

"I don't want to talk to you, Julian," he said.

"C'mon, Lonnie," I said. "Just hear me out."

That was the last sentence I got out before Howie Wartnose tackled me. I had no idea he was there. It turned out Quentin and Howie were walking about ten steps ahead of Lonnie. They'd just turned the corner, so I hadn't noticed them when I ran up behind him. I felt myself tumbling backward onto the front lawn of a house, with

Howie riding me down, and then I felt his full weight on my chest.

Now would be a good time to mention that I've never been in an actual fight. I know that sounds strange, but it's the truth. I don't think I have the personality for it. I get mad sometimes, for sure, like when I chased after Eduardo in the playground. But I was just going to tag him hard, not fight with him. What I mean is, when I do get mad, it's always an annoyed kind of mad, not a bug-eyed kind of mad. Lonnie even teases me about it . . . like, one time we were watching a couple of junior high school guys going at it on Union Street, and he nudged me with his elbow and said, "Why don't you jump in there, Jules?"

That's not to say I've never wrestled around with guys in a jokey kind of way, and for a second that's what I thought was going on when I felt Howie straddling me. It was only when I looked up and saw his eyes bugging out that I realized he was serious.

"Why'd you do it?" he yelled. But at the same time he yelled the words, he also started to drool. I noticed a droplet of drool form at the corner of his mouth, and I knew it was going to fall into my face. I twisted my head to the left just as it came loose. It must have missed me by an inch. "Don't you move!" Howie yelled. "Don't you move a muscle!"

The drool was gone when I looked back up. I eased back my shoulders and waited to hear him out.

As soon as he felt me relax, his eyes changed. It was slight but noticeable. The anger was still there, but there was hurt mixed in with it. "Why did you do it, Julian?"

"Do what?"

"You know what!"

"I don't, Howie."

"Why did you kiss Beverly?"

"What are you talking about?"

"You kissed her at the museum!"

"I didn't kiss her at the museum!"

"Then where did you kiss her?"

"Nowhere," I said. "I didn't kiss her."

"Then how come it's all over school?"

"I don't know."

"Tell the truth!"

"I'm *telling* you the truth, Howie. I buddied up with her at the museum because she didn't want to be stuck with Hank Feltscher. That's it. I don't know what you heard, but that's the truth. If you would've just asked me instead of getting weird about it, I would've told you."

"Let him up," Lonnie said.

Howie glanced back over his shoulder at Lonnie. "He's lying."

"He's not lying. Let him up."

Howie looked back down at me. "If I let you up, are you going to run away?"

I smiled up at him. "If I think you're going to hit me, I'm going to run away."

"You see!"

"Let him up!" Lonnie grabbed Howie by the shoulder and pulled him off me.

As soon as I felt his weight come off, I sat up but didn't stand. I looked him in the eye and said, "Howie, there's nothing between me and Beverly."

"Why should I trust you?"

"Because it's the truth," I said. "There's nothing between me and Beverly . . . *and there's nothing between you and Beverly.* I'm telling you the truth for your own good. This thing with her has been going on for too long. You've got to let it go. She doesn't want to be your girlfriend. That's not going to change."

"How do you know?"

I took a deep breath. "*Everyone* knows."

When I said that, I watched the light in his eyes go out. The anger went away. Even the hurt went away. There was nothing left except the glaze on the surface. He looked killed.

"I'm real sorry, Howie."

He ignored me and turned to Lonnie, which made

sense. That's who I'd want to hear it from if I were in his position.

"Is it true?" he said.

Lonnie exhaled. "What do you want me to say?"

"Just tell me if it's true."

"Yeah, Howie, it's true."

He said it quick and direct, like pulling off a Band-Aid.

Howie swallowed hard and turned to Quentin, his last hope. Quentin had his head down at first and wouldn't meet his eyes, but then he glanced up and nodded.

"Why didn't you tell me?"

He was still looking at Quentin, but he meant the question for all of us. I wanted to answer him, but I couldn't find the right words. There were no right words. There was no excuse. We should've told him. For his own sake and for Beverly's sake. We knew the thing was hopeless, but none of us said a word. Except behind his back. He was our friend, he was one of us, but we laughed about him and Beverly behind his back.

He spun around again and faced Lonnie. "Why didn't you tell me?"

Lonnie said, "Because guys don't take away other guys' dreams."

As he said that, he was staring straight at me.

Howie lowered his head and muttered, "You're not true friends."

"Yes, we are," Lonnie said. I thought he was going to say more, but that was all he had. There was a real painful silence afterward.

"Then how come you didn't tell me?"

"No one thought it would go on so long."

Howie turned and started up the sidewalk by himself. It was pathetic to watch. He wasn't quite running, but he was rushing to get away from us, with his shoulders slumped forward and his head hanging low. It was so pathetic that I wished I'd never opened my mouth. Quentin took a step after him, but Lonnie caught him by the arm. "Let him walk it off."

"He'll be all right," I said, standing up. "He just needs a little time."

"A *little* time?" Lonnie said. "Is that what you think?"

"He needs time to get over it. I don't know how much."

"But in your opinion a *little* time will do the trick?"

"I don't know how much time it'll take," I said.

"But you're in the *gifted* class. So maybe you can tell Quentin and me how much time it'll take Howie to get over it. I'm sure you can figure it out if you use your *gifted* brain."

That cut into me real deep. I wanted to tell him what I meant. I wanted to tell him what had happened with Jillian. But right at that moment, the best I could do was, "C'mon, Lonnie."

Then he said the worst thing he'd ever said to me, the worst thing *anyone* has ever said to me: "I don't want to have nothing to do with you ever again."

He kept staring me down, but after that I couldn't bear to look at him. I could feel my breath catching in my throat. There was a sick feeling in my stomach. I caught sight of Quentin out of the corner of my eye. He had an expression on his face that was pure confusion.

Then, at last, Lonnie turned to Quentin and said, "C'mon, let's get out of here. It stinks in this neighborhood."

They walked away, and I was left standing alone.

May 18, 1969

The Rabbi's Advice

Maybe for the first time, I'm glad I'm doing this assignment. Not because it's going to get me out of *Julius Caesar,* or not *just* because it's going to get me out of *Julius Caesar,* which is worth it no matter what. But because it's proof. I've spent the last three days reading over what I've written, page by page, sorting out what I did wrong that got me into this mess. Here's what I've come up with: I killed a bird. I caused a guy to crash the car he'd stolen (so that could count for *or* against me, if you think about it). Also, I did that thing to Danley Dimmel. But once you get past those three things, I did nothing wrong. I tried to be a good friend, to do unto others, etc. But what did I get in return? Grief and more grief.

It's getting to me too. I'm not sleeping well. I wake up

in the middle of the night rolling back and forth, driving my elbows into the mattress. Not even bawling, just mad. Mad at myself. Mad at Lonnie. Mad at Jillian. But you know who else I'm mad at when I wake up pounding the mattress?

God.

I know you're not supposed to say you're mad at God. You're not even supposed to *think* it. I feel low thinking it, but I can't get rid of the thought. Yeah, I know God's got bigger things to worry about than what's going on in my rinky-dink life. Like what's going on in Guatemala. What right do I have to be mad at God, given what happened to Eduardo? Now *there's* a guy who has a real beef with God. But he rolled with it. How rinky-dink do I look in comparison? That much I realize *logically*. But realizing something logically doesn't mean realizing it in your guts. Logically, I know it doesn't matter that Eduardo is going to beat me in front of the entire school on Track and Field Day. But deep down in my guts, it matters. It matters a lot. Why did God make Eduardo so calm about things? Why did God make him so fast? And why oh why oh why did God send him to P.S. 23?

Things came to a boiling point this morning in Hebrew school. If there was ever a worse time for a pop quiz, I don't know when it would be. To say that I wasn't in the mood is an understatement. Rabbi Salzberg broke the news a half hour before the end of class. He had this wicked grin on his face as he handed out the quiz, and I had to fight back the urge to crumple up the paper and walk out the door. Then he sat down behind his desk at the front of the room and peered down at us. He's got these wire-frame glasses with half lenses, rounded at the bottom and straight-edged across the top, so that even when he's looking straight at us, it always feels like he's looking down. Plus, he smells like old cigarettes and fish. I don't know if it's him or his suit, but it's a smell that stays with you, that hangs in the air. I couldn't breathe for a couple of seconds as I looked down at the quiz.

The first question was "Name the three patriarchs of the Israelites."

I thought about it and wrote down: "Lonnie, Eduardo, and Jillian."

Then I folded the quiz paper in half and rested my head on the desk.

It was maybe a minute later that I got a whiff of old cigarettes and fish. I looked up, and Salzberg was standing next to me. His glasses were halfway down his nose. He had a real annoyed expression on his face.

"Mr. Twerski?"

"Yes."

"Are you done with the quiz?"

"No, I'm just resting," I said.

"How far have you gotten?"

"Not very far."

"Let me see."

"I'd rather not, Rabbi."

"You'd rather not?"

"Let me finish first."

I unfolded the paper and started back to work. As I was about to read the second question, Salzberg snatched the paper away from me. I sighed to myself but said nothing.

He carried the paper to the front of the room. That wicked grin came back to his face as he told the class to put their pencils down. Then he said, "Who can tell me the patriarchs of the Israelites?"

For several seconds, no one answered. It had to be a trick. Then, at last, a kid named Ira Schwartz in the front row raised his hand. Salzberg called on him, and Ira said, "Abraham, Isaac, and Jacob."

"You are *wrong*."

"But—"

"According to Mr. Twerski, the patriarchs of the Israelites are Lonnie, Eduardo, and Jillian."

The class roared with laughter. I felt my face going red.

"Correct me if I'm wrong, Mr. Twerski, but isn't Jillian a girl's name?"

"Yes."

"Ah."

"I'm sorry, Rabbi."

"Why are you sorry? You've taught us a valuable lesson. You've taught us that a patriarch can be a girl . . . or perhaps even a Spaniard. Isn't Eduardo a Spanish name? *Spheradit?*"

"No, Rabbi."

"Eduardo *isn't* a Spanish name?"

"Yes, it's a Spanish name. No, it's not the name of a patriarch."

"So it's a joke to you, this quiz?"

"No."

"Abraham, Isaac, and Jacob . . . do you think they're jokes too?"

"No."

"Do you think Hebrew school is a joke?"

"No."

"What about your bar mitzvah? Do you think that's a joke?"

"No, Rabbi."

"Then what *is* the joke? I'm not getting it, Mr. Twerski."

"There's no joke, Rabbi. I didn't mean to write that."

"Does your hand have a mind of its own?"

The class roared again.

"No, Rabbi. That's not—"

"You're saying it's your hand's fault?"

"No, Rabbi. It's my fault."

"See me after class, Mr. Twerski."

So I sat with my hands folded, waiting for the class to end. When it ended, the rest of the students handed in their quizzes, and half a minute later it was just me and Salzberg alone in the room. He stood up from behind his desk, walked over to the door, closed it, and then sat down again behind his desk. He drummed his fingers on the top of the desk. I took that to mean he wanted me to say something, but I had no idea what to say.

Finally, I muttered, "I'm sorry, Rabbi."

"What are you sorry for?"

"I'm sorry for messing up the quiz."

"It was too hard for you, the quiz?"

"No, Rabbi."

"You didn't know the patriarchs?"

"I knew them, Rabbi."

"Then explain yourself," he said.

The way he said it got to me. Before I had time to realize what I was doing, I was spilling my guts—about writing the love letter for Lonnie, about getting outrun by Eduardo, about getting kissed by Jillian, about buddying up with Beverly Segal, about making Jillian cry, about getting knocked down by Howie Wartnose . . . and about losing the best friend I had in the world.

Salzberg listened to the entire story without interrupting

me even once. The only sign I had that he was paying attention was when he would nod his head every minute or so. But even if he'd fallen asleep in the middle, I still would've kept going. No way was I stopping until the end.

When I was done, I realized a couple of tears had leaked out. I wiped them from my cheeks and leaned forward with my hands folded.

"It sounds as though you have a lot on your mind, Mr. Twerski."

"Yes, Rabbi."

"Do your parents speak Yiddish?"

"No, Rabbi."

"Have you ever heard the word *schlimazel*?"

"Yes."

"Do you know what the word means?"

"I think it means 'idiot,'" I said.

"That's *schmuck* or *schmo* or *schmendrick*."

"I thought they were all the same thing."

"No, a *schlimazel* is a fellow who has a run of bad luck. So we say a *schlemiel* is the fellow who spills his soup. A *schlimazel* is the fellow the soup lands on. Do you see the difference? Listen to the word, Mr. Twerski: *schlimazel*. Next year, at your bar mitzvah, your loved ones will come up to you and say *mazel tov*. That much you know. *Mazel tov* means 'good luck.' The word *mazel,* by itself, means 'luck.' Thus, *schlimazel* means 'bad luck.'"

"Am I a *schlimazel*?"

"No, Mr. Twerski, you're just going through a *schlimazel* phase. I'm sure it will pass. It always does."

"What am I supposed to do in the meantime?"

He cracked a smile. "Watch out for the soup."

May 27, 1969

The Punch Line

Now here's the punch line to the entire thing: I'm reading *Julius Caesar.* It's sitting right on my desk, the paperback—right next to my notebook, right under my lamp. What a joke, huh? The class started going over it last week, and I was leaning back in my chair, thinking about how, whatever else I'd screwed up, I'd gotten out of doing the book report on *Julius Caesar.* That was the point, remember?

So at first I wasn't even listening to you, Mr. Selkirk. I was hearing the sounds of the words coming out of your mouth, but I wasn't paying attention to what you were saying. Except it's harder to keep that going than you might think. Sooner or later, the sounds of the words and the meanings of the words come together, and the sentences start to make sense. You blink your eyes and notice you're paying attention. It's like a reflex. You can't turn it off.

I can tell you the exact moment I got sucked in. It was when you were talking about how Brutus is different from the rest of the guys who kill Caesar, how the rest of them are out for themselves, but how Brutus thinks he's doing the right thing for Rome—even if it means stabbing his friend in the back. That got to me, the way you talked about it. The way a guy can hurt his friend by doing the right thing, or doing what he *thinks* is the right thing. I'm not saying this just to kiss up. I'm sitting at my desk, and I'm reading *Julius Caesar,* and every page is making sense. Like at the very end, when Brutus runs onto his friend's sword, and then Mark Antony finds Brutus's body and says:

> *This was the noblest Roman of them all:*
> *All the conspirators, save only he,*
> *Did that they did in envy of great Caesar;*
> *He only, in a general honest thought*
> *And common good to all, made one of them.*
> *His life was gentle, and the elements*
> *So mix'd in him that Nature might stand up*
> *And say to all the world, "This was a man!"*

That just wrecked me. It's like the John Henry cartoon all over, except with just words and not pictures. As I said the words to myself, I felt chills running through me. That's what it means to be a man. You do what you think is right, regardless of who it hurts, and whether it works out, because in the end you have to live with yourself.

I finished *Julius Caesar*, but, crazy as it sounds, I still wanted more Shakespeare. So I went back to that speech I had to memorize in fourth grade: "What a piece of work is a man!" I found my old notebook from Mrs. Graber's class, and then I found the sheet of paper with the speech. Sure, I had to look up half the words. Again. But even before I did that, I knew, just from the sound of the sentences, what Shakespeare was saying:

> *What a piece of work is a man! how noble in reason, how infinite in faculties! in form and moving, how express and admirable! in action, how like an angel, in apprehension, how like a god! the beauty of the world, the paragon of animals! And yet to me what is this quintessence of dust?*

That's life in a nutshell, if you ask me. You think you're the greatest thing going, the fastest kid in the school, the smartest kid on the block. You've got friends who look out for you, good parents, a nice room, and a decent stereo. Heck, you don't even have to do the Shakespeare assignment! You've got life pretty much dancing to your tune.

Well, that's what *you* think. . . .

Because one morning you wake up, and you realize you're no one special, you're nothing to write home about. Not even a big nothing. You're like a teensy-weensy speck of nothing . . . a "quintessence of dust."

Here's another way to look at it. Two weeks ago, I lost the best friend I ever had. Two weeks from now, I'm going to lose the forty-yard dash on Track and Field Day. I won't be the fastest kid in P.S. 23 . . . and it won't be just a rumor. The entire school will know the truth for themselves. But life will go on. Except, sooner or later, it won't. Then I'll be dead, and in a hundred years, or a thousand years, who's going to care?

You know how in math class, whenever you're adding or subtracting fractions, you're supposed to find the common denominator? The common denominator in life is that in a thousand years, none of us is going to be here. Even if I were still the fastest kid in P.S. 23, even if I were the fastest guy in the *world*, in a thousand years the result would be the same. I'd be dead and buried, and no one would remember or care. It makes me queasy to think about it, but whatever I do in sixth grade, whatever I do in junior high school and high school and college, whatever I make of myself, I'm still a quintessence of dust.

But here's the weird part. Knowing the truth frees you up. Or at least it frees you up if you accept it. Knowing that, in a thousand years, nothing you're doing or not doing will matter frees you up to do what your heart tells you to do. So I listened to my heart for a couple of days and nights, and I turned off my brain, and then, suddenly, yesterday, as I was sitting in English class, I knew what to do.

I walked right over to Jillian at the end of the period. She was still sitting at her desk, straightening up her desktop before lunch. She looked real pretty. She had on a pink-and-gray-striped dress. Her brown hair was even darker and shinier than usual, and she had a pink ribbon in it. I looked her straight in the eye and said, "Do you want to go to a movie on Friday?"

The question seemed to catch her off guard, or maybe just the directness of it caught her off guard. She looked down and went back to shuffling her papers. Then she glanced up at me again. She was interested, but she wasn't quite smiling. "What movie?"

"I don't know," I said. "Whatever's playing at the RKO Keith's."

"Would it be just the two of us?"

"I'm sure there'll be other people in the theater."

"But not Lonnie?"

"No," I said.

"I spoke to him about us. He said he doesn't care."

"Trust me, he *does* care. But it doesn't matter."

"But why would he say he doesn't care if he does?"

"Because he's a great guy. That's what I've been telling you."

"Then why are you asking me to go to the movies on Friday?"

"Because it doesn't matter. He'll get over it. Or else he won't."

"But he's your friend."

"You don't have to remind me, Jillian. I know he's my friend."

"I don't want to come between—"

"Do you want to go to the movies with me or not?"

"You're supposed to act nicer when you ask me that," she said.

That was when I realized I was ruining it for her. "I'm sorry."

"Is this the first time you've ever asked out a girl?"

There was no reason to lie to her. "Yes."

"Friday is Memorial Day. We don't have school. You know that, right?"

"Why does that matter?"

"Your family doesn't do stuff together?"

"Not that I know of," I said.

She hesitated another second. "All right."

"So you're saying yes?"

"Where and when do you want to meet?" she asked.

"How about the RKO Keith's at seven-thirty?"

"Are we going to dinner first? Or should I eat at home?"

"Which would you rather?"

She cracked a smile. "You *really* haven't thought this through, have you?"

"I want to go to the movies with you, Jillian. Do you want to go with me?"

"I do."

"Then let's go," I said.

"What about dinner?"

"Why don't you eat dinner at home and then meet me afterward?"

She thought it over. "If I get my dad to drop me off, do you think your dad will drive me home?"

"I'll ask him."

"If he can't, will you ride the bus back to Bayside with me?"

"If it comes to that," I said.

"Do you promise?"

"I promise that you won't have to ride the bus home alone."

She put out her hand. "Then it's a date."

As I shook her hand, I was thinking, *I'm a quintessence of dust with a date for Friday night.*

June 1, 1969

Date Night

An hour after I asked Jillian to go to the movies, I began to ask myself, *What did you do that for?* That's what happens when your heart gets out in front of your brain. Your brain catches up, except by then there's nothing to do but scratch your head. Still, it wasn't like I was going to take it back. Sooner or later, I was going to have a first date. Why not Jillian Rifkin?

So, no, I didn't want to take it back. I just didn't want to think about date stuff. Like what movie we were going to see. Like whether twelve dollars, which was how much allowance I'd saved up, would be enough to buy tickets, popcorn, and sodas for both of us. Like whether I was supposed to kiss her good night.

If you step back and analyze the thing, of course, you'd

have to say the main reason I asked out Jillian was because I was mad at Lonnie. There's no dodging it. Which, I guess, makes me a double louse. I'm a lousy friend to Lonnie. And I'm a lousy boyfriend to Jillian. Writing that word feels weird: "boyfriend." Even thinking about it feels weird. It feels like a pair of dress shoes that doesn't fit, the kind where your feet are swimming around inside so you have to put on two pairs of socks and then pull the laces real tight, and you wind up with blisters below your ankles. I'd never thought of myself as anyone's "boyfriend." But if the first date went well, and if we went out on another date, then you'd have to say I was Jillian's boyfriend.

The thought made me kind of queasy.

Between Wednesday and Friday, I spent hours and hours going through the date in my mind, trying to work out every possible way it could go. But there were too many *if-thens*. Like with popcorn, for example: *If* she wanted popcorn, *then* should we both wait on line for it, or should she get us good seats while I waited on line? But in that case, after I bought the popcorn, how would I find her in the dark theater? Stuff like that. The kind of stuff you don't have to worry about if you're going to the movies with the guys because then you can just yell out one of their names, and he'll call back and wave his arms, and you'll call back to him, and who cares if the grown-ups sitting around you start going, *"Shhhhh!"*

I would've given my right arm—not really, of course—to talk it out with Lonnie, to get his take on things. But that was out of the question since the date was with Jillian. Not to mention that he wouldn't give me the time of day. It killed me every morning, waiting for the bus, the way he walked right past me without even a glance. Between him and Howie Wartnose, I was public enemy number one. Eric the Red and Shlomo Shlomo weren't as obvious. They'd at least nod hello. Still, you could tell they felt weird about it. The only one who stuck by me was Quick Quentin. But I don't think he has it in him to hold a grudge.

So I was flying solo.

Sure, I *could've* talked it out with my dad. That's how the world works on TV. . . . You know, the son sits down with his dad to get the facts of life. No question he would've razzed me, but he would've cut it out once he realized I was desperate. Talking to him also would've solved the problem of getting Jillian home after the date. I came close on Friday morning. I woke up an hour early and walked with him the three blocks to Thirty-First Avenue, where he'd parked the car the night before. The entire time, I was just about to spill my guts. I even got into the car with him, and he asked me what was on my mind. But I couldn't answer him. I couldn't get that first word out. I sat there and shrugged. He drove me back to the house without asking again.

If I couldn't talk to my dad about the date beforehand, I sure couldn't ask him to drive Jillian home afterward. Which meant I was going to ride the bus back to Bayside with her. That much, at least, was settled.

So I decided to let it go. Whatever happened, happened. I stopped thinking about *if-then* and focused on being a quintessence of dust. Would it matter in a thousand years what happened on my date with Jillian? What was the worst thing that could happen? I mean, if I pissed my pants in the movie theater, would it make a difference in a thousand years? People will be riding around in flying cars, going from planet to planet, and taking pills that let them watch movies inside their brains. Who will remember the kid who pissed his pants in the RKO Keith's?

By Friday afternoon, I didn't just *feel* like dust. I *was* dust. I could taste it in the back of my throat. There was dust in the corners of my eyes, and I could hear it blowing around in my ears. I could feel the wind coming up behind me and carrying me forward, light as dust, from the present to the future, and I had no more control over where I was going than a tumbleweed rolling across a desert.

Late in the afternoon, I took a quick walk over to the RKO Keith's to find out what films were playing. It turned out there were two possibilities: *Nightmare in Wax* or *Mackenna's Gold*. Both started at eight o'clock, so either

worked since we were supposed to meet at seven-thirty. I
stared at the marquee for a full minute. I didn't care, to be
honest, but girls don't like horror movies, or at least they
say they don't like horror movies, which nixed *Nightmare in
Wax.* So that left *Mackenna's Gold,* which was a western. If
nothing else, I figured there would be a tumbleweed in it.

Then I went home and tried to act as though nothing
was going on. I told my mom I'd be out later than usual
but no later than eleven o'clock. She likely figured I'd be
over at Lonnie's house watching television or trading baseball cards or doing whatever we did when we were together. She had no reason to ask questions, and she didn't.

But after dinner I ran into trouble with Amelia. She's
always been able to read me, and when I took extra time
in the bathroom—I mean, it was no more than a couple
of extra minutes to comb my hair—she parked herself outside the door and waited for me to come out. She cracked
up as soon as I opened the bathroom door. She took one
look at me, and she just knew I wasn't going to Lonnie's
house.

"You've got a girlfriend, don't you?"

I pushed past her. "Leave me alone."

"I'll bet it's that Jillian girl," she said.

"Get lost!"

I hustled back to my room with her footsteps right
behind me. But then, at once, her footsteps stopped. I shut

the door to my room and listened for her, but there was no sound. It was weird. If she'd followed me the entire distance, I would've slammed the door in her face—which would've caught the attention of my mom and dad. But she kept them out of it. She kept the thing between the two of us. She had me dead to rights and let me off the hook.

I cracked open the door and peeked out. She wasn't there.

Now *I* was curious. I should've let it pass, probably. But I couldn't figure out what had stopped her in her tracks—I mean, since she'd started to give me a hard time, but then just quit. If I didn't find out, the question was going to gnaw at me the entire night.

I walked the length of the apartment and knocked on her door.

"Who is it?" she called out.

"It's Julian."

"Julian who?"

"You know who it is!"

"All right. Come in."

I opened the door, which let in a breeze and rattled the beads on the wall. She was sitting cross-legged on her bed with a copy of *Newsweek* in her lap. There was no chance she was reading it. She hadn't been back in the room more than ten seconds before I knocked on the door.

I shut the door behind me.

"Maybe I do," I said.

"Maybe you do what?"

"Maybe I have a date."

"With Jillian?"

"Yes."

"It's nothing to be ashamed of."

"I'm not ashamed of it," I said.

The right corner of her mouth turned up. "What I mean is, you don't have to feel awkward about it. It's the most natural thing in the world. It's not the kind of thing you have to hide."

"I'm not hiding it. It's just not a big deal."

"Are you nervous?" she asked.

"No."

"You're sure you're not nervous?"

"Why should I be nervous?"

"You're not even slightly nervous?"

"Whether I'm nervous or not, what does it matter? I'm not going to chicken out."

"You make it sound like an ordeal, like a math test. But it's not like a math test."

"I know that," I said.

"I don't think you do," she said. "You can screw up a date just like you can screw up a math test. But it's also different because there's not one right formula. You see? You don't have to study for it because there are lots of right formulas. You just have to be yourself and pick the one you can make work."

I nodded. I had no idea what she meant.

"Let's start with the basics. What are you going to wear?"

"Just a shirt and pants. What I wear to school."

"If you wear jeans, wear a *nice* pair. All right?"

"All right," I said.

"And a nice shirt, with buttons. Oh, and no sneakers."

"All right!"

"Did you take a shower?"

"This morning."

"Did you put on deodorant?"

"Just now, yes."

"What kind?"

"The kind Dad uses," I said.

"You used Dad's Mennen?"

"I didn't think he'd mind."

"Well, first of all, *ick.*"

"Why?"

"I'm only joking, Julian."

"Oh."

"Now, let me smell you—"

"C'mon, Amelia!"

She lunged forward before I could react, grabbed me by the waist, and sniffed my underarms. I felt stupid standing there, letting her do it, but I wanted to know if there was a problem. She let go of me a moment later and fell back onto the bed. Then she squinted her eyes like she was deciding whether I stank.

"Well?" I said.

"Not bad."

"What else?"

"Did you brush your teeth?"

"I will before I leave."

"What about your tongue?"

"What about it?"

"You have to brush your tongue too," she said. "You have to go all the way back with the toothbrush until you gag."

"Then why is it called a toothbrush?"

"What?"

"Shouldn't it be called a tooth-and-tongue brush?"

"Don't be such a wiseass," she said, smiling. "Are you going to a movie?"

"Yes."

"What movie?"

"Mackenna's Gold."

"Not a superb choice, but at least it's not a horror movie. You're planning to pay for her, right?"

"Yes."

"How much money do you have?"

"Twelve dollars," I said.

"How did you manage to save that much?"

"I stole it from your purse."

"What did I say about being a wiseass?"

She jumped up again and walked over to her dresser. She pulled open the top left drawer and rummaged around. After a couple of seconds, she came out with a twenty-dollar bill and shoved it into my palm.

"Why are you being so nice to me?"

"Because when you're grown up, you're going to think back to your first date, and you're going to remember it was on Memorial Day in 1969. You're never going to forget the time or the place, Julian. I guarantee it. But here's the thing. You're also going to say to yourself, whenever you think back, 'Amelia came through for me.' I know that doesn't make sense right now, but when you're grown up, trust me, it will. Now, let me give you a few more pointers."

"I'm not stupid—"

"No, but you're passive."

"I'm not passive!"

"You don't take charge. You let things happen."

"That's not true," I said.

"Isn't it?"

"No, it isn't."

"You let Lonnie make too many of your decisions—"

"He *doesn't* make my decisions."

"He got you suspended," she said. "I don't know exactly what happened with that boy down the block, but I know it must have been Lonnie's doing. Everyone who knows you knows that, Julian. Even if you won't admit it."

I tried to say calm. "*Lonnie does not make my decisions. The two of us just think alike. There's a big difference,* Amelia."

"Look, I think it's fine that you and Lonnie are friends. You've known the kid for your entire life, and now he's the leader of the pack—I get that. But you have to be your own person. Even if the two of you think alike, you have to separate yourself. You have to go your own way, figure out who you are without Lonnie around."

"You're just like Dad! You *hate* the guy!"

"I don't hate Lonnie, Julian. I'm sure he has good qualities. But he's also the kind of guy who'd pick on someone who can't defend himself. You have to face that fact."

"Danley Dimmel can defend himself! Have you ever seen him?"

"He's *slow,* Julian. He goes to a special school. You and Lonnie both know that—"

"Why are you always talking Lonnie down?"

"I'm not talking him down. I'm talking *you* up. You're not a little kid anymore. You're going out on your first date tonight—"

"Which Lonnie has nothing to do with."

"Good!" she said. "Then *take charge!*"

She shrugged at me in a sarcastic way, as if she'd just made her point. I wanted to answer her, but the conversation was going downhill. That's par for the course with Amelia. You start talking about one thing, and then, without warning, you take a sudden turn into the Amelia zone, and you're done. She means well. The proof was the twenty-dollar bill I was clutching in my palm. But you couldn't reason with her, not once she got an idea in her head. She had a low opinion of Lonnie, and nothing I said was going to change her mind.

I turned and walked out of her room without another word. But then, like a minute later, I was back in my room, going over the conversation, and I started to feel guilty. I glanced at the twenty-dollar bill, which was now folded in with the rest of the money on my desk. I thought about the fact that she hadn't razzed me, that she hadn't said a word to Mom or Dad. Then I thought about how she'd come through for me with the dying pigeon, and how she always came through for me, and how I'd walked out of her room just now without even a thank-you.

I walked back to her room and knocked on the door.

"You're welcome," she called out to me.

"Thank you," I said anyway.

"Just be yourself, Julian. Except not a twerp."

*   *   *

By seven-thirty, I was standing out in front of the RKO Keith's, waiting for Jillian to show up. The sun was almost gone, but there was still a sliver of light casting shadows along Northern Boulevard. Loud honking was coming from a big traffic jam at the intersection of Northern and Main Street. Half the cars were trying to turn left onto Main Street, the other half left onto Northern, but no one was giving an inch either way.

I had a bad feeling in my gut, looking at the long line of people outside the theater waiting to buy tickets. What if *Mackenna's Gold* was sold out? I didn't have a backup plan. I started to count the people waiting out front and stopped when I got to thirty-five, not even half the line, because I suddenly realized that I had no way of knowing how many of them were there for *Mackenna's Gold* and how many for *Nightmare in Wax.*

Most of the people looked high school age at least, maybe even college age. There were families too—a dad and mom and their three daughters were right at the front of the line. The oldest of the three daughters looked about my age, which made the feeling in my gut worse. Who did I think I was fooling? Twelve-year-old kids don't go out on dates on Friday nights. The only way they wind up at the movies on Friday nights is with their parents.

That was what I was thinking when I heard Jillian call

my name. I turned around in time to see her father drive off in a sleek red car. I saw him in the car before I saw her. He gave me a quick wave, just a back-and-forth swivel of his hand. I started to wave back but stopped myself. It wasn't the kind of wave you're supposed to wave back at. I just nodded instead.

Jillian rushed up to me and grabbed me by the hand. She had on a light-blue dress with pink and white flowers, which made me feel wrong because I had on jeans. *Nice* jeans, like Amelia said, but still jeans. Not creased pants. If a girl puts on a flowery dress for a date, she deserves creased pants. Jillian didn't seem to mind. She squeezed my hand real hard. Except then she said, "Let's not do this."

That stunned me. "Not do what? Do you want to go home?"

She smiled in a real sly way. "Let's not go to the movies."

"Why not?"

"The line's too long. Plus, I've got a better idea. Unless you already bought the tickets. If you already bought the tickets, I don't mind going."

"I didn't buy the tickets yet."

"Then let's go to Adventurers Inn," she said.

That stunned me a second time. "Adventurers Inn?"

"I want to ride the roller coaster."

"But it's like a mile away."

"C'mon, we can walk it—"

"I know we can walk it, but why should we?"

"C'mon, *please!*"

I gave the idea a couple of seconds of thought. From the sound of her voice, I knew she was going to be thinking about Adventurers Inn the entire time we were watching *Mackenna's Gold*. Plus, I liked a roller coaster as much as the next guy. So why not go with the flow? If going with the flow made me a twerp in Amelia's eyes, then I guess I was a twerp.

"All right, let's go to Adventurers Inn."

Jillian lunged at me and gave me a big hug. It was embarrassing, her doing that in front of the long line of people. I didn't hug her back. I just stood there, stiff as a parking meter, and likely with the same stupid glass-eyed expression. I stared straight ahead and waited for her to calm down. She did maybe a second later, and then I started to walk back along Northern Boulevard in the direction of Linden Place. She followed a couple of steps behind, but then she sped up until we were walking side by side. That's how we went for the first block. But I knew what was next: she made a grab for my hand. I felt her hand in mine, and I took it. No one was paying attention at that point, so I didn't mind.

"You're sweet," she said. "Nothing ever bothers you."

I just shrugged at that. What else could I have said?

Adventurers Inn was a straight shot down Linden Place. It's a long walk and not a nice one. It starts out nice enough at Flushing Town Hall, on the corner of Northern and Linden, which is like a huge reddish-brown castle with arched windows and balconies and flagpoles. It looks real official, except nothing ever happens there. I've never seen the front doors open, not even once. But I think the building goes back at least to the Civil War, so it's not like it's going to get knocked down.

Town Hall is the first thing you see on Linden Place. The street starts at that corner. So you look at Town Hall, and you think you're going to take a grand historical walk with landmarks and stuff, but it goes downhill pretty fast. After that first block, it's vacant lots and deserted gas stations and auto parts stores with loose tires out front and walls covered with dirty graffiti. There are rows of private houses too, but none you'd want to live in. Their front lawns look like junkyards. Except in junkyards, there's stuff you might want to buy. Here you've got rusted-out refrigerator doors, smashed toilet seats, and kitchen sinks. That sounds like a joke, but it's true. You've got actual kitchen sinks sitting out in front of people's houses. Plus, it's not a safe neighborhood. You have to watch out for muggers. But they tend to stay away on weekends because there's more traffic, and cops cruise by every so often.

Jillian got more and more nervous as we went along.

Not that she would admit it. But the last of the daylight was gone. The streetlights were on, which cast shadows and made the sidewalk glow yellow. She was glancing from side to side, squeezing my hand tighter and tighter. It got to a point where I turned to her and said, "Don't worry. I know where we're going."

"I'm just maybe cold," she said. "I'm not worried."

"We could take Union Street, but it's much longer."

"No, I want to get there the quickest way."

That was the last we spoke for quite a while. I didn't feel too awkward about it, which might sound strange, but the fact that she was nervous made the silence more bearable. I felt like I had a job to do—get her to Adventurers Inn. I couldn't be bothered with keeping up a conversation at the same time. It was another ten blocks before we came to Whitestone Lanes, which is where Linden Place livens up again. There were cars pulling in and out of the parking lot, plus at least a dozen people standing around on the sidewalk outside the bowling alley. That relaxed Jillian. She let go of my hand, which I appreciated because both our palms were sweating.

I pointed to the Whitestone Expressway overpass. "Adventurers Inn is just on the other side of the highway."

"Really?"

"Look, you can see the top of the Batman Slide—"

"Where?"

"That line of green lights." I pointed them out.

"I see them!"

She grabbed my hand again, but just for a second. Just to let me know she was grateful, or at least, that's how it felt to me. I was feeling pretty good right then. I'd gotten us to Adventurers Inn by the shortest route. So even if I'd been a twerp in one way, I'd taken charge in another.

We hurried through the underpass, which had a foul smell, and then out to the main gate, right in front of the glowing yellow sign that read ADVENTURERS INN. The place was jammed. There was a long line at the entrance, though it was more like a mob that was moving in the same direction than an actual line. It narrowed as you got closer, and there was a lot of glaring back and forth as people sorted out who was in front of who.

It was a ten-minute wait to buy a ticket. The entire time, we could hear screams from inside the park. Lots of them sounded fake. In my experience, the loudest scream- ers are high school girls. Not because they're scared, but because it's what's expected. You rarely hear little kids scream. They may cry if they get scared, or beg to come down from a ride, but they don't scream.

The park tickets cost three dollars each, which wasn't bad, but I had to fork over another twelve dollars for two night passes so that we could hop on whatever rides we liked without standing on line to buy tickets every time.

That meant I was out eighteen dollars before we walked through the gate. I was thankful for the twenty-dollar bill Amelia had slipped me.

People always talk about the sights and sounds of an amusement park, about the rainbow-colored lights and buzzing neon signs, or the rows of purple and pink and red stuffed animals, or the barkers in black top hats yelling their lungs out, or the swirling organ music, or the pop songs piped in once the rides get going. Or else they talk about the crowds, about the fat old guys leading their families around, or the teenage guys in sleeveless undershirts, or their dates in tank tops and short shorts, or the little kids who get so caught up in the sights and sounds that they bonk into one another and start to bawl. But the smells are what get to me. You've got your hot dog smell, your popcorn smell, your cotton candy smell, your cigarette and cigar smell, your ladies' perfume smell—plus, there's that gear-grinding, metal-on-metal smell from the rides. You've got all the smells mixed up together, and it's like walking in a cloud. If I live a hundred years and I never go back to Adventurers Inn, I'll still remember those smells.

"Isn't this better than a movie?" Jillian said as we strolled along the midway. We'd only been inside the park for a minute when she said that, but she was right. There was no denying it.

"It's kind of a real-life movie," I said.

"Are you having a good time?"

I nodded that I was, which was the truth.

"What do you want to do first?" she asked.

I glanced left and right. "How about the Ferris wheel?"

Her expression went sour. "Really?"

"The line's not too long—"

"But once you're up there, you're *up there*. Then what?"

"You sit back and take in the view," I said.

"Then let's do that last. It's the perfect last thing to do."

"What do *you* want to do first?"

"How about the Music Express?" she said.

"Sounds good to me."

The Music Express is just your basic ride, nothing special. It goes round and round on a banked track, except it's speeded up because the purpose is to throw the riders inside each car together. High school guys like it because it's an excuse to get cozy with their girlfriends. But it's also fun to ride with your friends since whoever sits on the right gets crushed against the side of the car. I found that out the hard way the first time I rode the thing with Quentin and Lonnie. I thought the two of them were going to come right through my rib cage and wind up on the other side of me.

The line at the Music Express didn't look too bad. There were maybe a dozen people waiting at the gate. The song

"Dizzy" was blaring from the ride's loudspeakers, louder and louder as we got closer. But as soon as we came to the back of the line, Jillian started standing on her toes for a clearer look at the front. Then she started to wave.

"What are you doing?" I asked.

"Looking for someone I know."

"Who?"

Before she could answer, a skinny blond guy in a black Adventurers Inn T-shirt waved back at her and began making his way toward us. The way he was cutting between people, sliding in and around them, and the fact that no one was giving him a hard time told me he wasn't just another guy waiting on line.

"Hey, babe!" he called as he stepped past the last three people and walked up to us. He gave Jillian a playful shove. She shoved him back, and then he winked at her. I doubt he meant for me to see the wink, but I saw it. Right then, I got a bad feeling.

"Hi, Devlin."

Devlin turned to me and put out his hand. He had the skinniest, boniest fingers I'd ever felt, but he squeezed my hand real hard. It was painful, like getting squeezed by a skeleton.

"I'm Julian," I managed.

He let go of my hand only after I'd told him my name. It felt like he'd squeezed it out of me.

"Devlin mows lawns on my block. He started last week. He goes to McMasters."

"You're in seventh grade?"

"Eighth," he said. "You?"

"Sixth."

"Ouch!"

"Tell me about it," Jillian said.

"You'll grow out of it, though." Devlin laughed real loud and gave Jillian another playful shove. She shoved him back harder, and then he waved his hands at her, as if to say he surrendered.

"Julian is writing a book."

"You're kidding me! What kind of book?"

"It's not a book," I said. "It's just something I'm doing to get out of Shakespeare."

"Is it more than ten pages?"

"Yeah."

"Sounds like a book to me!" He laughed real loud again.

"Devlin's brother runs the ride. That's him standing at the gate."

"Oh."

"So Devlin rides for free," she said, "as many times as he wants."

"Yeah, it's pretty cool," Devlin said. "I hang out with him on the weekends. I've ridden the thing hundreds of times, so I'm pretty sick of it. But it's still a sweet gig. I get to eyeball the chicks. You know how it is."

"You're so *bad!*" Jillian said.

Right then, the Music Express came to a halt, and the cars started to empty out. The people behind us surged forward and pushed us to the front of the line. I took out the two passes and flashed them at Devlin's brother—who looked just like Devlin except taller and bonier and with pimples on his chin. He put out his arm as Jillian and I were about to step past him.

"How old are you?"

"Twelve," I said.

"Got to be thirteen."

"What?"

"Got to be thirteen to ride unaccompanied."

"But I've ridden it before with my friends."

"Not at night you haven't," he said.

"What's the difference—"

"C'mon, Duane," Devlin said, "I'll ride with 'em."

Duane glanced down at his brother with the fakest look of surprise I'd ever seen. Then he hesitated and rubbed the pimples on his chin, like he was giving the situation another thought. Maybe a second passed before he said, "All right, if you ride with them. But just this once."

Devlin hopped up the three steps to the Music Express

and put out his hand for Jillian. I followed a step behind. He helped her into the car and then climbed in after her. The two of them squeezed together to make room for me on the right side of the car. The squash seat. I glanced at Jillian, but she wouldn't meet my eyes. What could I do at that point? I slid down into the seat and stared straight ahead.

It took maybe another minute for the rest of the cars to fill up. I could hear safety bars slamming down and latching, and parents telling their kids to hang on tight to the bar, and right behind us a couple of high school guys were wisecracking about throwing one another off the ride once it got going.

Then, at last, Duane called out, "Is everybody ready to rock and roll?"

Three or four carriages let out a halfhearted "Yeah . . ."

Suddenly, Devlin jumped up and yelled, "My brother said, 'Is everybody ready to rock and roll?'"

That got the entire ride to scream back, "Yeah!"

"That's better!" Devlin yelled, and then wedged himself back in between me and Jillian.

"I can't believe you did that!" she said. She elbowed him in the ribs. He was so skinny, and we were squeezed in so tight, that I could feel the jab of her elbow.

The music started up, real loud, and right in the middle of the song:

Indian giver!
Indian giver!
You took your love away from me!

The Music Express lurched forward, and we were off. Jillian began to shriek with excitement. I don't know how else to describe the sound she made. You could go to the end of a piano and not come close to how high her voice got. Meanwhile, Devlin was pounding his bony hands on the safety bar to the rhythm of the song and singing. I couldn't hear him. I'm not sure if he was singing the words out loud or just to himself. But I could see his lips moving. Red, white, and blue lights began to flash around the track as we picked up speed. There was nothing gradual about it, though—we picked up speed in sudden jerks, and each one of them snapped our heads back.

It wasn't long before the ride was going full tilt. The music was beating inside my head, the lights were flashing in my face, and I was helpless. Jillian and Devlin were screaming their lungs out, letting go of the safety bar, and waving their hands in the air. Each time they let go, I could feel their full weight ramming against my left side. It was painful, like getting rammed by a sack of bones.

I closed my eyes and waited for the thing to end.

"C'mon, man!" Devlin screamed in my ear. "Be free!"

I opened my eyes and nodded at him.

Then I heard Jillian scream, "C'mon, Julian!"

I nodded at her too. I had no idea how else to react.

The ride went on for maybe two minutes but felt a lot longer. I felt sick—not from the ride but from the situation, the fact that I'd been set up. Suppose I'd bought the movie tickets before Jillian had ever showed up at the RKO Keith's. Would she have sat through *Mackenna's Gold* with me and forgotten about Devlin? But the more I thought about it, the less I cared. That sounds pretty bad, but it's the truth. I was back to thinking of myself as a "quintessence of dust," and the thing about a quintessence of dust is that it rolls with the breeze. However the breeze blows, whichever direction, the dust comes along for the ride. Which is also true of a twerp. So Amelia had me dead right. I was a twerp. I was the quintessence of a twerp.

By the time the ride jerked to a stop, my left side ached from my shoulder down to my hip, but I felt nothing whatsoever about the situation with Jillian and Devlin. What I *did* feel was relief. The date was over. I was just curious how she was going to make it official.

The answer came after the three of us climbed out of the car. I hopped down the steps of the ride ahead of them. I didn't turn and wait for them because I thought they might be holding hands—which would make things even more awkward. Out of the corner of my eye, I noticed Duane give a thumbs-up sign to Devlin. But I still didn't turn around.

Then I felt Jillian's hand on my shoulder. "Did you have a good time, Julian?"

That forced me to stop and turn around. Devlin wasn't with her. He was back by the gate of the Music Express, talking with his brother. People were streaming past us on both sides. It seemed pointless, the two of us standing there, about to have a conversation neither of us wanted to have. All we were doing was parting the crowd.

"It wasn't my favorite ride," I answered.

"Didn't you like the music?"

"It's not my favorite song either."

"Julian . . ."

I pretty much knew what she was going to say, but I didn't care. "Yeah?"

"Do you mind if Devlin hangs out with us?"

"No, but—"

"He's a fun person. You'll see."

"What I was thinking was that I'm not much in the mood for Adventurers Inn. I might go home. But the two of you can use the passes. Here . . ." I shoved the passes into her hand.

"Really?"

"Why not? I won't be using them."

"That's such a sweet offer, Julian."

Devlin jogged up behind us right then. "Where to next?"

"Julian's going home. But he's going to let us have his passes. Isn't that the sweetest thing?"

"That's real cool of you, man. *Real* cool."

He put out his hand, and I shook it. He didn't squeeze as hard this time.

Jillian stepped forward and gave me a long hug, and then the two of them turned and walked off in the direction of the Ferris wheel. They hadn't gone more than ten feet before he slipped his arm around her shoulder. Her arm slid around his waist, and that was the last I saw of them as they disappeared into the crowd.

That was when I heard a familiar voice. "I'm so sorry, Julian."

Eduardo was standing right behind me. I spun around to face him. He looked as if he was about to bawl . . . for my sake.

"*¡Qué lástima, Julian!*"

"What are you doing here?"

"She told me you asked her to come to the movies," he said. "But I knew she wanted to come here. I told her it was not a nice thing to do—to ask you to come here."

"It's not a big deal," I said.

"It was not a nice thing that happened. *¡Qué lástima!*"

"What does that mean?"

"It means 'what a pity.' It is a pity her heart is with him."

"That was the feeling I got."

"Maybe not forever," Eduardo said. "I hope it is not forever. He wears shirts with no sleeves, and he curses very much, and in front of grown-up ladies too. But that's where her heart is, and where a woman's heart is, you cannot argue."

"He's all right. Give him a chance."

"You have a generous soul, *Julian*."

"No, I'm a twerp."

"I don't know this word 'twerp.' Tell me, what does it mean?"

"If you look it up in the dictionary, you'll see a picture of me."

He smiled. "So you are making a joke. It's a very brave thing."

"It's not brave—"

"Soon, though, when you win first place, maybe the hurt will be less."

I looked him straight in the eye. "You mean on Track and Field Day?"

"Yes, of course—"

That made me laugh. Despite everything, that made me laugh out loud.

"What is so funny?"

"That's not going to happen. I'm not going to win. We both know it."

"No?"

"*You're* going to win," I said.

That cracked him up. "I don't think so, *Julian*. But maybe I will. No one knows what will happen because it is the future. But it will be an honor to run against you. That much I am sure of."

He put out his hand, as usual, and I put out my hand. But instead of a regular handshake, he slid his palm forward and wrapped his thumb around mine. It was like the two of us were making a fist together. I'd seen high school guys shake hands like that. It felt like a grown-up thing to be doing.

He said, "It will be a good race, I think."

"If you say so."

"It *is* what I say."

I was about to walk off, to cut my losses and call it a night, but then I had another thought. "I told Jillian I'd ride home with her on the bus. Do you think Devlin will take her home?"

"I will make certain she is safe, *Julian*."

June 13, 1969

Track and Field Day

One good thing and one bad thing came out of my "date" with Jillian at Adventurers Inn. The bad thing was that Jillian told whoever would listen that Devlin was her new boyfriend. The week before, she'd told whoever would listen that I was her boyfriend, so kids who'd never said a word to me were tapping me on the shoulder in the hall and telling me how sorry they were that I got my heart broken. That's a no-win situation. You nod and smile, and they think you're bawling on the inside. You roll your eyes and shrug, and they think you're acting like a jerk.

The good thing that came out of the date with Jillian happened as I was walking home from school Monday afternoon. I'd just gotten to Parsons Boulevard when I heard footsteps come up fast behind me. It was a sound I would've known anywhere, anytime. It was Lonnie running to catch up.

He slapped me on the shoulder. "I *knew* she was no good!"

"No, I was an idiot for going."

"How much did you lay out?"

"Eighteen dollars," I answered, "for the two of us."

Lonnie gave me a pained look. "You laid out eighteen bucks, and then she walked off with another guy? That's about as low as you can get. Where'd you come up with eighteen bucks?"

"Amelia loaned me some of it. Or maybe she gave it to me. I'm not sure."

"It gets worse and worse! 'Cause you *know* she's not going to let you pay her back. You're going to owe her a favor, and it's going to wind up costing you a lot more than eighteen bucks. Mark my words—"

"I don't think it's like that, Lonnie."

"Just mark my words," he said. There was a long pause as we continued to walk. He started to speak a couple of times but stopped himself. Then, at last, he said, "Look, I'm sorry I got a little crazy. I went screwy in the head. I wish it didn't happen, but it did happen."

"We both got a little screwy."

"No, I shouldn't have treated you like I did. You didn't do a thing wrong."

"I asked Jillian out," I said. "I shouldn't have done that, regardless."

He grinned at me. "That *was* a pretty screwy thing to do, looking back."

"Then we're good?"

"Yeah, we're good."

Just like that, we *were* good. I know how that sounds, but it's true. It's not as if the memory goes away. I'm not saying it does. But life goes on, and Lonnie is still Lonnie, and I'm still me, so what's the point of dwelling on the past?

"Are you going to beat that guy or what?"

"What guy?"

"You know . . . *Eduardo.*"

"I don't know, Lonnie."

"C'mon, you've *got* to beat him!"

"He's real fast."

"I don't care if he's real fast. He's a dirtbag."

"He's *not* a dirtbag."

"Then how about the fact that he's Jillian's fake brother? Are you going to let Jillian's fake brother beat you? Are you going to give her that satisfaction after the way she treated you? Are you going to give her that satisfaction after the way she treated *us*?"

"What if there's nothing I can do about it?"

"There is something you can do about it," he said.

"What?"

"Run faster."

So that was the strategy I had going into Track and Field Day: *run faster*. What other strategy is there? The thing about sprinting is there's not much to think about. You listen for the gun. You push off. You run as fast as you can until the end. Either you're fast enough to come in first, or you're not. That's what I like about it. It's pure. But it's also terrifying for the same reason. If you're not fast enough to come in first, you're not going to come in first. There's no way to come in first except by running faster than whoever comes in second.

The school year was winding down. Another week passed, and another weekend, and I spent the entire time studying for tests and thinking about losing to Eduardo. Studying was by far the less painful thing to do. I don't know if I was ever more prepared to take a bunch of tests. I aced every one, including English. (Thanks for the 96, Mr. Selkirk!) The last one came on Wednesday, June 11, in social studies. Before I turned in my test paper to Mr. Loeb, I wrote at the bottom, "Sorry again about what I said to Mr. Caricone. I deserved to sit out in the hall. Sincerely, Julian Twerski, the second-fastest kid in P.S. 23."

I stared at the words after I'd written them. There was no shame in being the second-fastest kid in school, even if the fastest kid was a fifth grader. That just proved it was a fluke case. He was a fifth grader, but he was two years older than I was, and bigger and stronger, so after it was over I could still say, and not be lying, that I'd never lost to anyone my age or size.

But then a thought came to me that made me shiver: *What if I didn't even make it to the finals?* The way I had the thing pictured, Eduardo would sail through his heats, and I'd sail through mine, and then we'd end up racing in the finals, and he'd win, and that would be that. But at least the entire school would see how he towered over me, and how he kind of had a mustache, and how the race wasn't fair from that point of view. That would maybe take some of the sting out of it. But what if we wound up together in one of the first heats? No one would be paying attention at that point. The bleachers would still be filling up, kids would still be looking for their friends in the crowd, waving their arms and yakking. If Eduardo blitzed me in the first heat, no one would notice. The thought of losing in the first heat was unbearable.

That meant I had to avoid standing near Eduardo as the runners were grouped. The problem was that the rest of the runners were going to avoid standing near me for the same reason. So, in a way, I did have a strategy.

I figured I'd take a long time in the locker room changing into my gym shorts and sneakers, maybe even make an extra trip to the toilet, then head across the street to Memorial Field at the last minute and show up as Mr. Greetham was counting off the first heats. I knew Eduardo was the kind of guy who stepped forward as soon as he was asked. So if I could sneak into the very last group, we wouldn't meet until the finals. Mr. Greetham would be looking around for me, on account of last year, so even if I got to Memorial Field a minute or so late, he'd squeeze me into that last group.

Track and Field Day came on Friday the thirteenth. I hung around after social studies period talking to Mr. Loeb. He told me right off he hadn't graded the final exams yet, but I told him I just had a question about social studies. Then I asked him how come the class was called "social studies" and not "world politics" or "world history" or "world geography"—which, when you think about it, was what we learned in that class. He took that question and ran with it. I remember listening to the sound of his voice, but I didn't hear a word he said. I kept thinking about the gym shorts and T-shirt tucked under my arm.

The conversation with Mr. Loeb, if you want to call it that, took maybe five minutes, and then I headed downstairs to the boys' locker room. It was jammed with fifth and sixth graders changing their clothes, which made the old dirty sock smell stronger than usual. There was a lot of yapping back and forth, bragging without meaning it, griping about teachers. That kind of thing. Two guys moaned real loud when I walked through the door—like they'd been praying I wasn't going to show up. I also got a quick nod from Willie, the guy who finished second to me in the finals last year. I nodded back at him and then made a beeline for the last toilet stall at the rear of the locker room.

That was where I changed. Afterward, I just stood in the stall with my school clothes tucked under my left arm and listened. There's a big difference between listening to guys when you're looking at them and listening to them when they're just voices. You pick up more when it's just their voices. You start to hear not only what they're saying but their mood. Even guys I didn't know, I could tell from the tone of their voices whether they thought they had a chance to make it to the finals or whether they were running just for the heck of it. Most of them were running just for the heck of it. That killed me—how they knew they were going to lose, and how after they lost they'd just shrug, walk back across the street, change back into their school clothes, and nothing would be different for them. You could almost think of the scene at Memorial Field like a painting that was about to be painted, with guys in the background and guys up front. The guys who were running for the heck of it were in the background. The guys up front were Eduardo and me.

I waited for the entire locker room to clear out, and then I waited another couple of minutes just to be safe. When I opened the door of the stall, it was eerie how quiet and still it was. There was a gray sock dangling out of the bottom of a locker, stuck between the frame and the door. It caught my eye, the way it was all twisted and mangled. I felt bad for it. It was a stupid thought. I mean, it was just a gray sock. But the thing looked like it was in pain.

I waited as long as I could in the locker room and then headed out to Memorial Field. The walk took about half a minute, and I arrived as Mr. Greetham was dividing up the guys into heats. Just as I thought, Eduardo got picked for the first heat. So did Willie, which made me feel bad. He was like that gray sock, in a weird way. About to get mangled by Eduardo. I could've warned him to avoid Eduardo's heat. But then he would've realized what I was doing.

Mr. Greetham shot me a where-have-you-been look and then penciled me into the last heat. There were only four of us in the last heat. The other eleven heats had six runners. The winner of each heat advanced to the semifinals—twelve runners in all. Then the top two finishers in each semifinal—four runners—raced in the finals.

As Eduardo and Willie lined up for the first heat, I was feeling real guilty. I *should've* warned Willie to avoid that heat. He was a good guy. He'd given me a quick hug and whispered "Good race!" after I beat him in the finals the year before. He still smiled at me whenever we passed in the hall. If the situation were reversed, if he knew about Eduardo and I didn't, he would've warned me.

There was nothing I could do now but watch.

Eduardo towered over Willie and the other four runners at the starting line. It wasn't fair. He was just too big. He looked like a camp counselor who'd rounded up his campers and forced them to stand in line. Then he did something I'd never seen before, at least not in person. He got down into a sprinter's crouch—like the runners do in the Olympics. Willie glanced over at him with a confused expression on his face. It looked weird, not just the fact that Eduardo had gotten into a crouch but also the fact that he looked even bigger and faster hunched over than he did upright. The way his shoulders were pointed forward, the way his hair was trailing down his neck, he looked like a racehorse. It caught the attention of pretty much everyone at Memorial Field, even the kids in the stands. The yakking stopped. It was like someone flipped a switch. Not only could you hear the hush—you could feel it.

"Runners ready!" Mr. Greetham yelled.

Willie and the rest of them leaned forward. Eduardo didn't flinch.

"Set!"

Eduardo raised his head slightly.

"Go!"

Eduardo rocketed off the starting line. He was ahead by three steps almost before the other runners got going. His arms and legs were churning together in perfect rhythm. There was no wasted effort. He began to straighten up, and his stride began to stretch out. My heart beat faster and faster as I watched.

But then a miracle happened, or at least it seemed like one to me. Willie stayed with him. Eduardo still had that three-step lead, but he wasn't pulling away. My heart started to pound even more. It was pounding as if I were running, not just watching. Eduardo and Willie were out by themselves . . . and then Willie started *gaining* on him. Willie lowered his head, and Eduardo's three-step lead became two steps, and then one step. Then Willie let out a yell. I remembered that yell from the year before. He'd yelled as I pulled away from him in the finals. Back then, I thought he was yelling out of frustration. But now I realized it was because he was going full speed, putting his guts into the race. He was dead even with Eduardo now, and the two of them were hurtling together toward the finish line. . . .

Willie beat him by a step.

Yeah, I know how plain and dull that sounds, *Willie beat him by a step*, but I don't know how else to say it—maybe because at first I couldn't even make sense of what had happened. I could still hear the echo of Willie's scream in my ears even though he was walking calmly now, with his hands on his hips, ten yards beyond the finish line. I could feel, but not quite hear, cheers coming from the students in the bleachers. I watched Eduardo jog over to Willie and shake his hand.

Then, just as the world clicked back into place, I heard Mr. Greetham call out the time: "Five-point-one."

Five-point-one?

I'd run four-point-nine twice as a fifth grader and coasted at the end. How could that be faster than Eduardo? Then again, the way Eduardo was running, how could Willie have caught and passed him? It wasn't possible. Except I'd seen it with my own eyes. But the time had to be wrong. *Had* to be wrong. That was the only explanation I could come up with. No way was that a five-point-one. Mr. Greetham had read the stopwatch wrong, or maybe the stopwatch was broken.

But the times for the rest of the heats sounded right— five-point-seven, five-point-six, five-point-eight. That was the range for the next nine heats. After the first six, I couldn't watch them anymore. I listened for Mr. Greetham to start each race, and then I listened for the time. I felt exhausted and sick to my stomach, so I closed my eyes and waited for my turn.

I heard Mr. Greetham call, "Heat twelve, to the starting line."

I opened my eyes and walked onto the track.

I heard a girl in the bleachers yell, "That's him! That's him!"

But I didn't turn around. I focused on the track crackling under my feet as I stepped up to the starting line. The chalk was smudged from the first eleven heats. The longer I stared at it, the blurrier it looked. The wind was blowing in my face, not hard, but enough to make me think, *I'm a quintessence of dust.*

I heard Mr. Greetham yell, "Runners ready!"

I tensed up, then relaxed.

"Set!"

I took one deep breath.

"Go!"

The weird thing is, I don't even remember running the race. I remember pushing off, and then taking one hard step, and then grunting, and then nothing. Not even the rush of wind. The next thing I remember is running past Mr. Greetham, who was standing at the finish line.

Then, a second later, I heard his voice: "Four-point-seven."

When he called out the time, a loud cheer came from the crowd. The sound of it washed over me, and I knew what it was for, but it felt wrong. It felt like a joke. *I* felt like a joke, like a fake. When I thought I was going to lose, I'd told myself there was no difference between being the fastest kid in the school and the second-fastest. I'd told myself that I was a quintessence of dust whether I won or lost. I'd talked myself into it. Except now I was going to win. What difference did it make? I was still a quintessence of dust. I was a quintessence of dust who'd run a four-seven forty. But still a quintessence of dust. Out of the corner of my eye, I noticed the other three runners in the heat walking off the track with their heads down.

"I'm sorry," I said, half to them and half to myself.

Then I heard Greetham again. "Why'd you slow up?"

I turned to him and said, "I'm sorry."

"Don't be sorry. Just run through the finish line."

As I was jogging back to the starting line for the semis, I saw Jillian jumping up and down in front of the bleachers, waving her arms at me. I started to wave back, except then I noticed Devlin standing next to her—he must've ditched school. I lowered my head and jogged past them, but Jillian yelled out my name.

I took a deep breath and walked over to her. "What?"

"Julian, that was *so* amazing! You're *so* fast!"

I was shaking my head. "It doesn't matter. . . ."

"It *doesn't matter?* I've never seen anyone run so fast."

I shrugged at her.

Then Devlin said, "Maybe next year, when you're in junior high, I'll race you."

The way he said that, for some reason, just cracked me up. I started to laugh.

"What's so funny?" he yelled.

"I'm sorry," I said, but I kept cracking up. I couldn't help myself.

"I'll race you right now! You think I won't? I'll race you right this minute!"

The more he yelled, the funnier he sounded. I was laughing in his face, which I guess he deserved, but I was also laughing at myself, at what a fake I was. I turned and started to walk back toward the infield.

"You're a punk!" he yelled. "You're nothing! Did you hear me? You're nothing!"

I called back to him, "Maybe you're right. But I can outrun you backwards."

He kept yelling, but I couldn't hear the words anymore.

I looked up and saw Willie standing and smiling with the rest of the semifinalists near the starting line. He stepped forward as I jogged over to them. "Four-point-seven, huh?"

"I'm sorry," I said.

"What are you sorry about?"

"I don't know."

He laughed at that, even though I didn't mean it as a joke. I couldn't bear to look him in the eye after I hadn't warned him, after I'd let him race the first heat against Eduardo.

"You know what?" he said. "I think I might run a four-point-six . . . just to see what it feels like."

"I hope you do."

Except he *wasn't* going to run a four-six. He'd just run the race of his life at five-one. He was never going to know what a four-six felt like. That was the truth, whether he knew it or not.

But then at once I realized: *I* could run a four-six. I could run it for both of us. Willie deserved to run it more than I did. He deserved to know what it felt like. But the world doesn't care who deserves what. The world doesn't care, period. It had coughed up two quintessences of dust, me and Willie, and I could run a four-six, and he couldn't. There was no rhyme or reason to it. It was just how things had worked out. If one of us was going to run a four-six, it would have to be me. Maybe, then, it wasn't *exactly* true that nothing mattered. Maybe what mattered was doing what you could do . . . for the sake of the guys who couldn't do it themselves.

I wasn't going to let Willie down.

Mr. Greetham separated me and Willie for the semis. I'm sure he did it on purpose since we had the two fastest times. None of the other ten runners had broken five-point-five. So Greetham put Willie in the first semifinal and me in the second. I smiled at Willie and wished him good luck as he walked to the starting line. He ran a good race, and he pulled away at the end, but without Eduardo to push him, I knew the time wasn't going to be as fast.

Greetham called out, "Five-point-three."

I looked down. . . . I couldn't bear the thought of how bad I was going to beat him in the finals.

Then Greetham called out, "Next semifinal, to the starting line."

As I walked to the line, I had one thought: *I'm going to run a four-six.*

That was the thought that carried me through the race, the reason I pushed myself not to ease up at the end even though the race wasn't close. I bore down and leaned forward as far as I could crossing the finish line. Then I held my breath and waited for Greetham to call out the time.

"Four-point-seven," he said.

The kids in the bleachers cheered again.

I turned to Greetham and stared at him. "But I didn't slow down!"

"You got ragged at the end. The effort was right there, though."

"I want to run a four-six."

"That's going to be tough. You've run two races already."

"I'm *going* to run a four-six."

He got a big grin on his face. "Then don't *talk* about it. *Do it!*"

There were four runners in the finals. I had no idea who was going to finish third or fourth, but I knew Willie was going to finish second and I was going to finish first. I also knew I was going to run a four-six . . . *because I could.* Greetham gave us a couple of extra minutes to catch our breath before he lined us up again. While we were standing around, Lonnie called my name from the edge of the bleachers. He waved me over. I glanced around to make sure I had time, then walked over to him.

"You crazy son of a gun," he said. *"Four-point-seven."*

"I'm going to run a four-six in the finals."

"So I guess Willie took care of Eduardo for you."

"Yeah, he beat him. I didn't think he would."

"It should've been you who put him in his place."

"For God's sake, Lonnie, let it go!"

"I don't mean nothing bad by it, Jules. You know I don't like the guy. Maybe I don't know him like you do. So we can agree to disagree if you want. But I'm not taking it back either."

I turned and started to walk toward the starting line.

Lonnie called after me, "You mad, Jules?"

"No," I called back, but didn't turn back around.

"Then get mad! Run that four-six!"

That's the thing about Lonnie. He's got his faults, for sure—I mean, the guy's only human. But he gets to the heart of the problem. I'd coasted in the first heat. I'd thought too much in the semis. I wasn't going to run a four-six unless I got mad. Real mad. Whether I got mad at Lonnie or at myself or at the world didn't much matter. I just had to get mad.

So I decided to get mad at the world. That was the biggest thing, and it included Lonnie and me, and even God, so I figured if I was going to get mad, I might as well get mad at the world. I mean, look at the way the world is. I don't even mean the huge stuff like earthquakes and disease and hunger. That kind of stuff is too awful to wrap your mind around. Or Eduardo's parents getting killed, or Lonnie's mom getting her tongue cut by the Nazis. If I got worked up about stuff like that, I'd feel like even more of a fake. Who am I to get mad at things like that? It would be like a mosquito getting mad at the cold weather. You don't like it, if you're a mosquito, but what the heck are you going to do about it?

What I got mad at was how things never seem to work out just right. Nothing in the world is ever perfect. It's like Shakespeare says: the elements are mixed. There's always a smudge somewhere that ruins it, whatever it is. You scrub and scrub, but you can never quite get rid of the smudge. Plus, even if you *did* get rid of it, you'd remember that it used to be there, and then *that* would ruin it. What I mean is, nothing is ever pure.

Except running a four-six in the final.

Four-point-six seconds. Forty yards.

That would be a pure thing. Time is pure. Forty yards is pure. Running is pure. If I ran a four-six, that would be that. It would be done and perfect, like a diamond. No smudge. I could tuck it away, and it would always be there to remember and think about and hold on to when the rest of the world got to me.

I wanted it bad.

Willie was waiting with the other two runners back by the starting line. The three of them were chatting, which I doubt they would've been doing if they thought they had a chance.

"You sure you want to run this race?" Willie called to me.

I smiled at that. "Yeah, I'm sure."

"The way you keep wandering off, seems like you've got other things on your mind."

"No, just this."

"'Cause you *know* you're going to have to run your behind off."

"I know," I said, still smiling.

"I'm gunning for you, Julian."

"I know that too."

"We're *all* gunning for you—me and my new buddies Scott and Wayne. We're all three of us gunning for you. You better run your best race, or else we'll run right up your behind."

Right then, as weird as it sounds, I loved Willie.

"Runners to the starting line!" Greetham called out.

The four of us walked over to the starting line. Then we waited. None of us spoke again, but Willie did this thing with his legs, kicking them out to the side as if to get them as limber as possible. It was the first time I'd seen him do it, the first time I'd seen anyone do it. I thought about doing it too because it looked like it might serve a purpose, but I didn't want to steal Willie's move.

Then Greetham yelled, "Runners ready!"

I took a deep breath and held it.

"Set!"

I said to myself, *Four-point-six.*

"Go!"

From the first step, I was out in front. After maybe six steps, I was clear. I couldn't hear the runners behind me. For a split second, but not even a split second, I almost eased up, but I caught myself and began saying, *Four-point-six, four-point-six, four-point-six.* As I said it over and over, the beat got faster. As the beat got faster, I felt myself running faster. *Four-six-four-six-four-six.* Way back behind me, Willie started to yell. It was the bravest, most hopeless yell ever. It sounded as if he was yelling for my sake, letting me know the race was over, telling me to run that four-six for both of us. I put my head down and began to yell too, straining in a way I never had before, straining with my legs but also with my guts and my throat. I was leaning forward, way out over my body, lunging toward the finish line. Then an instant later I ran past it, and I eased up and listened. . . .

Greetham called out, "Four-point-seven."

It felt like a stab in the heart when he said that. I looked up at the sky and took a deep breath. There wasn't a cloud anywhere, and the sun was washing across my face, and I was breathing hard in and out. I began shaking my head. Willie came jogging over to me. I heard his footsteps, and I turned to face him, but I couldn't bear to look him in the eye. He gave me a hug and said, "Nice job."

"I'm sorry," I said.

He laughed at that, then patted me on the back and jogged off.

I started walking away from the finish line, away from the rest of the runners and the cheers from the bleachers. I walked to the end of the track and then to the eight-foot fence that surrounded Memorial Field. Half a minute passed before the fact that I was still the fastest kid in school began to sink in. By then, I could hear kids from the bleachers spilling out onto the track, running across the infield, calling my name, asking me where I was going. It must've looked pretty weird to them because I was acting like I'd lost. They had no way of knowing I *had* lost. They'd heard Mr. Greetham call out "Four-point-seven." It was just a number to them. If he'd called out "Four-point-six," their reaction would've been the same. To them, the difference between four-seven and four-six was nothing.

To me, it was like a stab in the heart.

I stood at the fence, with my back to Memorial Field, and felt sick about what a fake I was. I knew it wouldn't be long before Lonnie or Jillian or maybe even Greetham came up behind me and asked me what was wrong. I was trying hard to snap out of it, to pull myself together.

That was when Eduardo showed up on the other side of the fence. He came out of nowhere, just like he had at Adventurers Inn. I put my arm over my eyes and pretended to wipe sweat from my forehead. But it was no use. As soon as I looked at him, a couple of tears leaked out.

"You are unhappy to be the winner?" he said.

I coughed. "I thought you were going to win."

"No, you are much faster."

"But I couldn't catch you."

"I *am* hard to catch, *Julian*. For many years, I have

played *fútbol*. I am very fast and very tricky, and very hard to tackle when I have the ball. But in a race, without a ball, you are faster. I thought you knew."

That made me smile, despite how I felt on the inside. "I didn't know."

"Still, you should be happy you are the winner."

"I wanted to run a four-point-six."

"What time did you run?" he said.

"Four-seven," I said, "all three races."

"That is very fast, *Julian*."

"But not fast enough."

He paused for a second, then said, "*Now* I understand."

"I don't think you do, Eduardo."

"You wanted to run a perfect race."

"I wanted to run a four-six, whether it was perfect or not."

"Then we will borrow *Señor* Greetham's stopwatch, and I will time you next week. If you do not do this thing next week, we will try again the *next* week. And if not then, the *next* week. The summer is long. It is not an impossible thing to do." He got a big grin on his face. "Then, afterward, I will teach you how to dribble. You will love *fútbol*. It is a beautiful game. You will love it very much, I think, *Julian*."

That cracked me up. The way he said it cracked me up. *He* cracked me up.

"You're a real fifth grader, Eduardo."

"*Sí, Julian*. I am . . . until September."

I shook my head at him, which made him smile. Then I turned and jogged back toward the infield.

Well, I guess that's it, Mr. Selkirk. I've kept this thing going longer than I ever thought I could, and I've learned a lot about myself and about life. I even read and liked *Julius Caesar*. So I've learned a lot about Shakespeare too, which should be a definite plus going into junior high in September. As for the summer, the only thing I know for sure is that I'm going to run a four-six forty if it kills me.

You can take that to the bank.

June 29, 1969

It's Not Fair . . .

I don't think it's fair, Mr. Selkirk. School is over. Next week is the Fourth of July. If you stop and think about it, you're not even my teacher anymore. So how is it fair that I have to keep writing? I've filled up nine composition books, which doesn't even count the work I did in the rest of my classes. *Nine composition books.* That's a lot of writing for a sixth-grade English class. That's a lot of writing for a *high school* English class, if you ask me.

I know I haven't written about what happened to Danley Dimmel, and I know that's the reason you haven't given me a grade, the reason you're making me sweat. Except you never said back in January that I *had* to write about it. You never said the words "You *have* to write about what happened to Stanley Stimmel." Maybe that's what you were thinking, but you never said the exact words. Because if you *had* said it, what if I'd said no? I'm not saying that I would have, but what if I had? It's like we had a deal, and we even shook on it, and then you changed it at the last minute. I mean, we *shook hands,* and I lived up to my end, and then you pulled the rug out from under me. Is that the kind of example a teacher is supposed to set?

Look, I'm sorry about what happened to Danley. Maybe I haven't said it outright, but that's what I was trying to say when I wrote "It's not like I meant for Danley to get hurt." That was the second sentence in the first composition book. I can bring it in if you don't believe me. I guess it's kind of weak, reading it back. I could've said I was sorry outright. But it's also the truth. I *didn't* mean for him to get hurt. It wasn't my intention. I did what I did, but I didn't know it was going to turn out like it did.

On the other hand, it's not like Danley's the first guy who ever got egged. You should drop by Thirty-Fourth Avenue on Halloween. Eggs are flying back and forth like it's a war zone. I've gotten egged. Lonnie's gotten egged. Shlomo Shlomo has gotten egged more times than I can even remember. It never crossed my mind that getting egged in December would be different than getting egged in October.

It never crossed Lonnie's mind either, or else he never would've mentioned the idea. I know that for a fact. He's a practical joker, for sure, but he's not cruel. You could even make the case that he was going out of his way to include Danley, that he was making him part of the group for a day. Like I said before, it's not like Danley has a lot of friends around here. He sits on his stoop at the end of the block, on the corner where Thirty-Fourth Avenue hits Union Street, twiddling his thumbs. Half the time, I swear, the guy's talking to himself. He lives on the block, but he might as well live on Neptune. It's sad that he's that way, but whose fault is it? Lonnie's? Mine? Danley is the way he is because that's the way he is. It's no one's fault.

Until last December, when the thing happened, the longest conversation I'd ever had with him was a couple of years ago when I said hello and he asked me if I wanted to play Battle. Just like that, out of the blue. That was the entire conversation. I said hello because I'd walked past him a thousand times, and it seemed stupid to walk past him over and over and never say hello, so I said it, and he looked up from his stoop, and then he said, "Want to play Battle?"

I had no idea what he was talking about. I just kept walking.

But it was such a weird question that it stuck in my mind. I mentioned it the next day in Ponzini, and Eric the Red said Danley had asked him the same thing. Same with Howie Wartnose and Shlomo Shlomo. It turned out that asking to play Battle was what Danley did. It was like his thing, like calling himself Danley instead of Stanley. Quentin said Danley asked him to play Battle every time he walked past him. The only guy he never asked was Lonnie, which made no sense either since Lonnie walked past him at least as often as the rest of us.

"You think he wants to fight?" Howie said.

"It can't be that," I said. "He's got this gooey look in his eyes."

Quentin nodded. "He definitely doesn't want to fight."

"Well, what the heck is he talking about?"

Then I had a thought. "Maybe he means Battleship."

Lonnie nixed that idea. "He doesn't mean Battleship. In the first place, you think a guy like that carries around paper and pencils? In the second place, it's too complicated. He doesn't have the brains for it."

We went back and forth for a few more minutes, but then we got sidetracked into a different conversation, and the subject never came up again. I thought about it from time to time, the weirdness of it, but I just chalked it up to the guy being slow—and maybe lonely too since he's never had a friend—so maybe he just doesn't know how to act.

Still, it's not like I had a grudge against him. I had no opinion about him one way or another. Except then, last

December, Lonnie came up with Scrambled Dope Day. How he came up with it, I'll never know. But that's the kind of thing Lonnie does. That's what makes him so interesting to be around.

It was a nothing of a Thursday morning, after Christmas and before New Year's. The entire gang was out back in Ponzini—Lonnie, Quentin, Howie, Eric, Shlomo, and me. The six of us were standing around with our hands in our pockets. I mean, it was freezing cold, and we were shuffling our feet to keep warm, and then out of nowhere Lonnie announced it was Scrambled Dope Day. That's it. Then he just clammed up. He wouldn't tell us what he was talking about. So we gave up asking and played wolf tag for a couple of hours just to fight off the cold, but our minds were on Scrambled Dope Day the entire time.

We had lunch at Bella Pizza on Northern Boulevard, and it was about the quietest hour we'd ever spent together because we figured any minute Lonnie would clue us in. But he still wasn't talking. By the time two o'clock rolled around, we were whining and yapping at him like a pack of wiener dogs, begging him to tell us about Scrambled Dope Day. Howie Wartnose pulled me aside at one point and said, "Shouldn't we be celebrating or something?"

That made me slap my head in disbelief. But still, I was dying to know what Lonnie had in mind.

It was about three-thirty when he gathered us into a

tight huddle in Ponzini and told us his idea: "Scrambled Dope Day is the day we egg Danley Dimmel."

I have to admit it was kind of a letdown. I don't know what I was expecting, but I wasn't expecting that. Except the more Lonnie talked it up, the more I got the spirit. Yeah, it seemed a little mean, given how Danley was. But getting hit by a few eggs never killed anyone, and Scrambled Dope Day sure sounded like more fun than standing out in the cold, doing nothing. Plus, Lonnie came at us with logic. His basic point was why should egging be just a Halloween thing? If it was all right to throw eggs the last day of October, why wasn't it all right the last week of December? And if it *was* all right to throw eggs the last week of December, didn't it make more sense to egg a dopey guy like Danley Dimmel than to egg each other?

Scrambled Dope Day might have been a bad idea, but Lonnie made a good case for it, and after a few minutes we were all in. Not that we had worked out the where and when and how. But Lonnie pulled out the five-dollar bill he kept in his shoe, which got us revved up, and said the eggs were on him.

"Not for long!" Howie Wartnose said, and the rest of us laughed because we knew what he meant.

As we started up Parsons Boulevard in the direction of Waldbaum's Supermarket, Lonnie took me aside and told me to stay behind. He told me he had a special job for me. It was up to me to get Danley to Ponzini. He told me to get him there in half an hour, not a minute sooner or later. He looked me straight in the eye and asked me if I could do that, and I told him I could. Then we synchronized our watches, and the rest of them headed off to Waldbaum's.

After they were out of sight, I stood on the corner of Thirty-Fourth and Parsons and tried to figure out how I was going to get Danley to follow me back to Ponzini. It wasn't a place he ever went. Like I said, he stuck to the stoop in front of his house.

I figured the first thing to do was talk to the guy. Maybe an idea would come to me. So I walked toward Union Street, and there he was, sitting out on the stoop, bundled up in a hooded sweater and jean jacket, staring down at the sidewalk. You can spot him a mile off because he's gigantic, and because he sits slouched over like he's watching the concrete dry. Except the concrete on Thirty-Fourth Avenue finished drying about a hundred years ago. But that doesn't matter to him. He sits on that stoop and stares straight down. I stopped right in front of his house, but he was so focused on whatever he was staring at that he didn't even notice me for half a minute.

That's when I said, "Hi, Danley."

He looked up and grabbed his chest like I'd almost given him a heart attack. He fiddled with his hearing aid for a second, maybe turning it on, or maybe just turning it louder. Then came that nasal voice of his. "You *scared* me."

"Sorry, I didn't mean to. I just wanted to talk."

That caused him to sit up straighter. "You want to talk to *me?*"

"Yeah," I said.

"What do you want to talk about?"

"You know who I am, don't you?"

"You live up the block."

"My name is Julian," I said.

He smiled. "I *know* what your name is."

"Oh."

"I'm not a retard, you know."

"Who said you were?"

"That's what people think on account of I ride the bus. But I'm not. It just takes me longer to get stuff. Maybe I'm not so smart, but I'm not . . . *that.*"

"I ride the bus too."

"Not the same bus."

"What I mean is, riding the bus doesn't make you . . ."

"What?"

"The thing you said."

He smiled like he'd never thought of it that way before. He took his hands out of his pockets and crossed his arms in front of his chest.

I said, "You're in junior high, right?"

That made him roll his eyes. "Yeah, eighth grade."

"You don't like it?"

"I don't like the teachers. They talk down to us."

"Then why don't you go to McMasters instead?"

"I take the test every June. It says I have to stay where I am. I guess maybe I *am* that thing."

"C'mon, you're *not* that thing."

"How do you know?"

"Because of how you talk."

"What do you mean?"

"You say words the right way."

"Like Stanley instead of Danley?"

"Yeah," I said.

"But I like Danley. It's different."

"Do you see my point? If you were that thing, you wouldn't think like that."

He waited for me to keep going, but I was drawing a blank. He got a weird look on his face that seemed to say two things at once, as if on the one hand, he couldn't figure out why I was talking to him, but on the other hand, he didn't want the conversation to end. Then, at last, he smiled at me and said, "Want to play Battle?"

"What do you mean?" I said.

"You know . . . Battle." He reached into his back pocket and pulled out a deck of cards.

"It's a card game?"

"Yeah. Didn't you ever play it?"

"I don't think so," I said. "What are the rules?"

"You put down a card, and I put down a card, and then whoever comes out higher wins."

"You mean like War?"

He shook his head. "No, *Battle*."

"I don't want to play Battle, Danley."

"Why not? My dad used to say a game of cards never hurt nobody. He used to play cards with me all the time. He doesn't live here anymore."

"What happened to your dad?"

"My mom kicked him out. But he used to bring me hot dogs with sauerkraut."

"Oh."

"Also, one time, he let me drink beer. I drank half a can of beer by myself. I could've kept going too, but he took away the can and drank the rest himself. Did you ever drink beer?"

"No," I said.

"It tastes *bad*."

"Then why did you drink it?"

"I don't know." He started to smile again. "I must be a retard, right?"

That cracked both of us up. He was laughing and shaking his head. For the first time, I felt kind of wrong about what I was doing.

"Why don't you ever hang out with us?"

He tilted his head to the side. "You mean with you and your friends?"

"That's right."

"Your friends play too rough."

"What are you talking about? You're bigger than the rest of us put together. If you played Johnny on the Pony, you'd kill us."

"I'm real strong," he said. "I weigh two hundred and eleven pounds."

"You'd break us in half!"

That got him laughing again, even harder than before.

"You should think about it. I could take you to Ponzini—"

"What's Ponzini?"

"That's the lot where we hang out. It's around the corner on Parsons."

"I walked up Parsons before," he said. "But I never saw a lot—"

"It's behind the apartment building. You can't see it from the sidewalk. That's the point."

"What do you do there?"

"Whatever we feel like doing. Whatever comes to mind. It's *our place.*"

He thought it over for a split second. He leaned forward as if he was going to stand up, but then he sank back down onto the stoop. "C'mon, let's play Battle. You could get good at it if you practice."

"Danley, it's freezing cold out. I'm not going to sit on that stoop and play cards."

"C'mon, I'll let you win."

Then, at once, I had an answer. "How about if we play tag first, and then we play Battle?"

That caught his attention. "Can we play Battle first?"

"It's too cold to play Battle first," I said. "We'll play tag first to warm up, and then afterward we'll play Battle."

"How long do we have to play tag?"

"Just until you catch me."

He laughed at that. "I can't catch you."

"How do you know?"

"I know how you run. Plus, look at me."

"Your legs are a lot longer than mine."

"C'mon!"

"You never know until you try," I said.

"I just have to tag you once?"

"Just once."

"And then we play Battle, right?"

"As soon as you tag me," I said.

"You promise?"

"I promise, Danley. As soon as you tag me, we'll play Battle."

He smiled and put the deck of cards down on the stoop. Then he stood up. I'd hardly ever seen him standing up, and for a second I got scared. There was just so much of him! His shadow seemed to go halfway up the block. Sure, he was shaped like a pear and had rounded shoulders. But if he jumped off the stoop, he'd be right on top of me. It would be like getting away from a falling tree. Once he took a step down, though, I relaxed. It was a slow, heavy step, almost like a slow-motion step. He took a couple of slow, heavy steps toward me, and I didn't move. I let him get real close, and then he lunged and I dodged him. He turned, laughed, then lunged again, and again I dodged him. He lunged a third time, and I jumped backward, then ran about ten yards up the block.

"Play fair!" he said.

I realized the tough part wasn't going to be dodging him. It was going to be letting him come close enough to think he had a chance of catching me. He had to believe that, or else he'd never follow me the entire way to Ponzini. Except after about a minute, he started to have a good time. I'm sure it was frustrating. But the thing was, how much exercise did he get sitting on that stoop? It was a change of pace. Plus, running after me was keeping him warm. His hands were out of his pockets, and he was flailing his arms, and the hood of his sweatshirt was flopping around behind his head, and he was making a noise that sounded like a squeal, except happier, probably because he was outside, off the stoop, playing like a regular guy.

Right then, I was even thinking that maybe he wouldn't mind too much getting egged. The eggs would wash off. I won't fake like he was going to be one of us afterward. He was too old, even if he wasn't the way he was. But at least he'd be the guy from the end of the block who got egged and took it like a man.

Meanwhile, the two of us were making pretty good progress. He'd chased me the entire length of Thirty-Fourth Avenue, and I kept it interesting by darting in and out of empty driveways and around rows of bushes. I stuck to the sidewalk. I never once ran him out into the street because you don't want to mix a guy like him with moving cars. The entire way, I kept glancing at my watch. By the time we made the turn at the corner of Parsons, I had three minutes left to get him to Ponzini.

So I sprinted ahead and hung a quick left into the alleyway that wound behind the building and led to Ponzini. He trailed me to the edge of the alleyway, then stopped in his tracks. He put his hands on his knees to catch his breath. For the first time, he had a suspicious look on his face.

I took several steps back toward him. "What's the matter? Did you give up?"

"Where are we going?"

"It's just Ponzini," I said.

"I don't want to go there."

"Why not?"

"I don't like it," he said.

"How do you know? You've never been there."

"Are your friends there?"

"Maybe, but I doubt it."

"But are you *sure*?"

"Look, do you want to play Battle or not?"

He'd caught his breath by then. He took a long look at me, sizing me up. I guess, looking back, right then was when he was making the decision to trust me. But that's not what I was thinking at the time. I was thinking I had another minute to get him back to Ponzini. I guess I should have thought about it more. Also, I shouldn't have lied to him about my friends not being there. That kind of stuff always seems clearer looking back. But how can you look back while the thing's happening? You can't. It's like you're on a ride, except it's your life. You can't call time-out, think it over, and then get back on the ride.

So, yeah, I did it. I shouldn't have done it, but I did. I turned and trotted down the alleyway, and a second later I heard his footsteps follow. I let him get close and then cut hard around the corner, and I heard his footsteps fall back, and then I slowed up again until he was right behind me, until I could almost feel his breath, and then, one last time, I tore out. I sprinted through the gap in the fence and into Ponzini.

The guys were crouched down together by the garage door, off to the side of the fence. I caught sight of them as I flew past, but I kept going. I didn't look back until I heard Danley yelling, "Oh no! Oh no! Oh no!"

By the time I turned around, the first eggs had hit him. It was just a barrage. Each guy was holding his own carton, grabbing out eggs and throwing them as hard and as fast as he could. Danley was staggering back and forth like a duck in a shooting gallery, not even ten feet from them, waving his hands in front of his face, begging them to stop, yelling, "Don't!" and "I give up!" and "No more!"

But the eggs kept coming at him, wave after wave. He tried to turn his back, but the guys circled around him and kept going. You could hear the thudding against his chest and sides and back. His entire upper half was scattered with eggshells and drenched in yolk. But the eggs kept coming and coming.

The thing was, he was such a huge target, and he was so close and so slow, how could you miss? The only misses I saw were a couple of eggs aimed at his face. That seemed like what he was most afraid of, getting hit in the face. He had his left hand in front of his face and his right hand cupped over his hearing aid, and he kept them there even though that left the rest of him wide open.

But then an egg hit him in the crotch, and you could hear the air rush out of him like a punctured tire, and he dropped his hands. Right off three eggs hit him in the face—one on his right cheekbone, one on his chin, and one on the bridge of his nose. He screamed and brought his hands back up, but a second later you could see blood between his fingers. I didn't know what to think. I mean, they were just *eggs*. How could eggs do that to a guy's face? It didn't occur to me that *that* was the difference between getting egged on Halloween and getting egged in late December. The eggs are harder, and your skin's colder and tighter. I realize that now, but I didn't realize it then.

I guess what I felt, watching it, was . . . amazed. I was too amazed by the sight to feel anything else. I know I should've felt something else. I know I should've *done* something else. But I just watched it. I watched them pelt the guy with eggs until their arms got tired, until he dropped down to his knees, let go of his face, and was crawling back and forth. Blood was dripping from his nose, and still the eggs kept coming and coming. I didn't do anything. I didn't say anything. I just watched it. How could that be? *I just watched it.* What I mean is, you could understand how the rest of them could get caught up in what they were doing. How their hearts could speed up and how they'd lose their minds. You could almost forgive it because they couldn't take a step back and realize what they were doing. But I *watched* it. I stood by and watched it. How could that be?

It kept going and going, and I watched it, and I didn't do a thing or say a thing to stop it. One by one, the guys were running out of eggs. Danley crawled over to the garage door and pressed his face against it. The last few eggs hit him in the back, and then the eggs stopped, and it was over.

Ponzini got real quiet—I mean, not even the wind was blowing. Except you could hear Danley sobbing. It was a sickening sound. We were watching him and listening to him, and the guys were huffing and catching their breath, and Danley must have sensed it was over because he turned around and faced us. He sat with his arms at his sides and his back against the garage door, and he was bleeding from cuts under his right eye and the bridge of his nose.

But then, out of nowhere, he started to smile. He was still sobbing, but I swear to God, the guy was smiling! You could see his teeth, and you could see blood on his gums and in the creases between his teeth, and you could see tears and blood mixing together and rolling down his face.

We were staring at him, all of us, and no one said a word for maybe ten seconds.

Then I heard Lonnie say, "Hey, Jules, think fast!"

I glanced up just in time to see him flip his last egg underhand in my direction. I caught it in both hands, and I held it. It was cold, but I could feel the yolk sloshing around inside.

"Your turn," Lonnie said to me.

I looked down at the egg and then up at Lonnie, and he was nodding at me, and I don't remember what I was thinking. But I looked at Danley, at how he was smiling, and I remember getting mad. I knew he didn't mean it, and maybe he didn't even know he was smiling, but there was something in that smile that got under my skin, and I felt the egg in my hand, and I knew it was a wrong thing to do, but I looked at Danley, and I looked at that bloody smile of his, and I threw the egg. I did it. I threw the egg. I knew it was a wrong thing to do, but I threw it anyway. It doesn't make sense. I knew it was wrong, but I threw it anyway. I reared back and threw the egg as hard as I could.

I missed him by about three feet. The egg hit the garage door about three feet from Danley's head and exploded. The shell disintegrated. There wasn't a trace of it stuck to the wood, and the yolk splattered like teardrops in every direction. It was a relief, to be honest, the fact that I missed, even though I knew I'd get teased, because I knew it was a wrong thing to do, and I knew, when I saw how the egg exploded against the garage door, how bad it would've been if I'd hit Danley in the face. I mean, as bad as I feel now, if I'd hit him, I'd feel that much worse. . . .

Why did you make me write this, Mr. Selkirk? To make me feel bad? Is that the point? Because if that's the point, then you win. I feel real bad. I did a wrong thing, a stupid thing. I'm sorry. If I could travel back in time, if I could live that day again, I wouldn't throw the egg. I wouldn't trick Danley into following me to Ponzini. I wouldn't go along with Scrambled Dope Day. But that's not how life works. You don't get do-overs. What do you want me to say?

I *know* what you want me to say. Both of us know what you want me to say. I didn't miss. I didn't miss. I reared back, and I threw the egg, and I threw it as hard as I could, and I didn't miss. I hit him in the mouth. I hit him right in the mouth. It was me! I'm the one who knocked back Danley Dimmel's teeth. It was me! What did I do? God help me, what did I do?

I knew it was wrong. I knew it was stupid. But I threw the egg as hard as I could, and I knocked back his teeth. The way he screamed . . . That scream is still in my ears. I can still hear it. *Right now,* I can hear it. When he started to scream, we ran away. We left him there, sitting against the garage door, with his teeth knocked backward, with blood pouring out of his mouth.

Lonnie yelled, "Cheese it!" and we ran away and left him there like that. I was the last guy out of Ponzini, but I was first through the alleyway and out onto the sidewalk at Parsons. I could've kept going. I could've run two blocks to Parsons Hospital and gotten help for Danley, but I ran straight home. God help me, I ran straight home. I ate dinner like nothing was wrong, and then I locked myself in my bedroom, and I thought I was going to vomit, but I didn't. I opened the window and felt a gust of freezing air against my chest. I thought about Danley still sitting against that garage door, sitting in the dark, with the blood frozen in his mouth, and I couldn't take it, so I told my mom I was going out for a minute. She gave me a weird look but didn't ask why, except she told me to put on my overcoat because it was ice cold outside. I grabbed a flashlight and ran downstairs and back to Ponzini. But Danley was gone. I found the smeared blood were he'd been sitting and a bloody handprint, and then I saw drops of blood that led out of Ponzini.

What did I do? What did I do? The guy never did a thing to me except want to play cards. He didn't even single me out afterward. His mom told the school that neighborhood kids did that to him, and then the guidance counselor made a PA announcement about an "incident." I think Victor Ponzini told his teacher who did it, and Ponzini's teacher told the guidance counselor, and the guidance counselor told Principal Chapnick, and then Principal Chapnick pulled us out of our classes and yelled at us and suspended us for a week, but that was it.

Danley never singled me out. He knew my name, for sure, but he never told. I did that to him, and he never told. What's wrong with me? Even when I passed him a week later, back out on his stoop, even when I saw him sitting there with black-and-blue welts on his face and with metal braces on his teeth, I didn't say I was sorry. I didn't say a thing. I just kept walking. I must have passed him on that stoop a hundred times since then, and I never said another word to him.

What's wrong with me? God help me, what did I do?

July 1, 1969

Dragging the Couch

The assignment is over, Mr. Selkirk. I'm done with it. If you want to flunk me, that's fine. Maybe I deserve to repeat sixth grade, but I can't keep writing this thing forever. I've got nothing more to say about what happened in Ponzini. That was last winter. Nothing's going to change it. Summer's here, and school's over, and I want to run a four-six forty and play soccer with Eduardo. What I mean is, I want to get on with my life. But I'm glad you made me keep going because you made me realize what I had to do.

The first guy I went to was Quick Quentin. I figured he'd be the easiest to convince, and I was right. I rang his doorbell, and he said yes as soon as I mentioned it. Before I mentioned it, almost. The second I said Danley's name,

Quentin started saying how the thing still bothered him, how he still thought about what happened whenever he looked at the garage door in Ponzini. He said apologizing would be a relief.

Quentin and I found Shlomo Shlomo and Eric the Red flipping baseball cards out in front of the Hampshire House, and the two of them said yes—though, to be honest, I think they said yes only because they were tired of flipping cards. Then the four of us found Howie Wartnose sitting out back in the playground, just twiddling his thumbs. He said no at first because he figured out it was my idea—he's still mad at me because of what I said about Beverly Segal—but Quentin talked to him alone for a couple of minutes, and in the end he said he'd apologize if Lonnie apologized.

That left Lonnie.

I knew he was going to be the toughest one to convince, but I figured he might go along if the rest of us were on board. The five of us went together and rang his doorbell. He came to the door, and he got a curious look on his face. There was a second—a *long* second—where no one spoke. Then at last I said, "Look, Lonnie, I've been thinking about what happened with Danley Dimmel—"

"Yeah?"

"So, the thing is, I think—I think we *all* think—we should apologize to the guy."

He started shaking his head. "No way, Jules. No way."

"C'mon, Lonnie," I said.

"That's ancient history."

"But it's the right thing to do."

"But what's the point?"

"It's the right thing to do."

"Look," he said, "I'm not saying I feel good about what happened. But here's the thing. We got yelled at, and we got suspended, and it's over and done with. Why dredge it up again? It's water under the bridge. I'm sure Dimmel's forgotten about it at this point."

"But I haven't forgotten about it," I said. "Neither has Quentin."

Lonnie glanced over at Quentin, and Quentin nodded.

"Then the two of you go ahead and apologize. You've got my blessing." He made a gesture with his right hand as if he was sprinkling us with water. "But leave me out of it."

That was when Shlomo said, "I think we should go as a group, Lonnie."

"Oh, is *that* what you think?"

"It *is* what I think," Shlomo said.

Then Eric said, "I think so too."

Lonnie turned to Howie at that point. "What about you?"

Howie took a deep breath and thought it over. "Well, it *was* your idea—"

"I knew it!" Lonnie yelled. "I knew it! You want me to take the blame!"

"It doesn't matter whose idea it was," I said. "You're missing the point."

"Then tell me what the point is."

"I already told you the point. It's the right thing to do. *That's* the point."

"Well, since you explained it like that . . . *no way, I'm not doing it!*"

When Lonnie gets that tone in his voice, he doesn't change his mind.

But then, a second later, I heard myself shouting. I don't remember deciding to shout. I don't even remember thinking the words before I started to shout them. It was as if the voice coming out of me wasn't me. What I heard myself shouting was this: "You said you'd drag a couch for me! That's what you said! You said you'd drag a couch down the street if I asked you!"

Lonnie's eyes narrowed down. "What are you talking about?"

The rest of them were staring at me like I was out of my mind.

"You said if I ever needed you to drag a couch down the street—"

Then, at once, Lonnie got it. He got it, and he started to laugh. He was shaking his head and laughing, and now the rest of them were staring at both of us, thinking we were *both* out of our minds.

"That's a pretty big couch you've got there," he said, still cracking up.

I looked him in the eye. "I know."

"You know it's one couch per customer. Next time, you're on your own."

"This is the couch that matters," I said. "I don't think the two of us can keep going without this couch."

He knew what I meant. "I wouldn't want a couch to be the end of us."

"Neither would I."

"Then let's do it," he said.

The six of us walked over to Danley Dimmel's house, and we found him sitting out on the stoop. I think he was scared for a second, but then he saw the looks on our faces, and that calmed him down. He still had braces on his teeth, but otherwise there was no trace of what we'd done to him.

Lonnie did the talking for us. He told Danley that the entire thing had been his idea, so he was the one to blame. But then I interrupted him and said I was as much to blame as Lonnie, and that got the rest of the guys stepping forward to take their share of the blame. I don't think Danley even knew what to make of it at first, but then he started to smile, and then he started to crack up. That made the rest of us crack up too. It was kind of comical, how we were falling over one another to take the blame.

Then Lonnie stepped forward and put out his hand, and Danley shook it. Then the rest of them did the same. Then it was my turn. I stepped forward, and I shook Danley's hand, and it felt like the rightest thing I'd ever done, the rightest moment of my life. If he had asked me to sit down on the stoop and play Battle, I would've done it. But he didn't ask. I stepped back, and he nodded at me, and I nodded at him. To be honest, I didn't know if we were nodding at the same thing. But I felt good and right and whole.

That's how it ended. Danley leaned back on his stoop, and the rest of us turned around and walked back up Thirty-Fourth Avenue. The sun was right in our faces, and I was squinting hard as we headed for Ponzini. What we did there, even though it was only yesterday, I don't remember.

Acknowledgments

Twerp would not exist without the interventions and ministrations of Charles Salzberg and Allison Estes of the New York Writers Workshop, Susan Altman of the Fashion Institute of Technology, and Scott Gould of RLR Associates. It wouldn't exist in its current form without the consistently gentle but shockingly perceptive edits of Chelsea Eberly of Random House.

This book is a radical departure from the ones that came before. For that, I am indebted to Linda Helble, along with Spencer and Spicy, who reminded me that I had a heart, and might want to consult it when I write.

About the Author

Mark Goldblatt is a lot like Julian Twerski, only not as interesting. He's a widely published columnist, a novelist, and a professor at the Fashion Institute of Technology. *Twerp* is his first book for younger readers. He lives in New York City.